**She looked into his piercing eyes.
"Oh, my God, we can't do this.
What am I doing here with you?"
She turned to walk away.**

He captured her hand and looked back. "This," he answered, and instantly she was back in his embrace. All caution flew to the wind. He kissed her quickly once, then again. Each time he paused for her reaction. The third kiss came. It was longer, languishing deep in passion and promise. When it ended they looked into each other's eyes. It was more than either of them could stand. The fourth kiss exploded and then there was more, so much more. There was a tangle of arms and bodies pressed together as one.

Reality had been eclipsed by the fantasy of his embrace. Jacqueline had never been so completely consumed by a kiss. Her response was instantaneous. She moaned deep in her throat. He gripped her tighter, pressing her close. He wanted her to know his arousal. She did, and knowing she had this power over him was exhilarating. All she had to do was…yield.

Books by Celeste O. Norfleet

Kimani Romance

Sultry Storm
When It Feels So Right
Cross My Heart
Flirting with Destiny

Kimani Arabesque

Love is for Keeps
Love After All
Following Love
When Love Calls
Love Me Now
Heart's Choice

CELESTE O. NORFLEET

is a native Philadelphian who has always been artistic, but now her creative imagination flows through the computer keys instead of a paint brush. She is a prolific writer for the Kimani Arabesque and Kimani Romance lines. Her romance novels, realistic with a touch of humor, depict strong sexy characters with unpredictable plots and exciting storylines. With an impressive backlist, she continues to win rave reviews and critical praise for her sexy romances that scintillate as well as entertain. Celeste also lends her talent to the Kimani TRU young adult line. Her young adult novels are dramatic fiction, reflecting current issues facing African-American teens. Celeste lives in Virginia with her husband and two teens. You can contact her at conorfleet@aol.com or P.O. Box 7346, Woodbridge, VA 22195-7346 or visit her website at www.celesteonorfleet.com.

Flirting With
DESTINY

CELESTE O. NORFLEET

KIMANI™
ROMANCE

To Fate & Fortune

KIMANI PRESS™

ISBN-13: 978-0-373-86190-3

Recycling programs
for this product may
not exist in your area.

FLIRTING WITH DESTINY

Copyright © 2010 by Celeste O. Norfleet

www.kimanipress.com

Printed in U.S.A.

Dear Reader,

Over the years I've learned that sometimes it takes more than luck to bring two people together. I love the idea of uniting unique characters in different ways. In *Flirting with Destiny,* I use superstition.

The heroine, Jacqueline Murphy, is superstitious. Black cats, spilled salt and, of course, the dreaded Friday the thirteenth all top her fearful list. And she's so used to fighting against her superstitions and all the bad things in her past that she can't see when something good is right in front of her—in this case, Gregory Armstrong.

Greg has his own dramas to overcome, but he knows a good thing when he sees it. Together they discover that love can happen when you least expect it to and that it's always right on time. Enjoy this journey with Jacqueline and Gregory as they discover love is their ultimate destiny.

Blessings & peace,

Celeste O. Norfleet

Chapter 1

When you look for trouble, you usually find it. Jacqueline Murphy saw trouble. She spotted him as soon as he walked into the reception. He was tall, well over six feet. He had a smooth, honey-kissed complexion and a strong, powerful build. His facial features were classic: firm, set jaw with just a trace of a mustache and goatee, bedroom eyes that hinted at more than his obvious African-American ancestry, and luscious, full lips that were setting her body on fire.

Yeah, he looked like trouble—the best kind. Tall, dark and handsome, he was what midnight fantasies were made of. Slow sex on a hot sultry night. However with her run of luck lately, this fantasy would turn into a nightmare. Still, there was a connection as soon as he noticed her. A quiver of nervous energy shot through her body. It had been a long time—too long, her sister would say. But she kept her focus, and it wasn't going to be on him. She'd been putting out fires all evening. This was one fire she'd just have to let burn itself out.

She looked around the room. The list of near disasters was long, but she still decided to chalk the evening up as a success. The private birthday reception she'd organized was going extremely well. Everyone seemed to be having a great time. She'd even gotten a much-coveted "two thumbs up" from the newly reelected Mayor Newbury himself. Of course no one had a clue that the fresh flowers arrived ten minutes before the doors opened, the caterer completely changed the menu at the last minute, the band's truck ran out of gas on the highway and two bartenders called in sick. But she handled it. It was her job. As the special-events planner for the city, she took chaos and created perfect order. She sometimes even got involved with city planning and management policy. She did it all.

All this was exactly what she intended to remind the mayor. She needed—no, she *deserved*—a raise and a full-time assistant. Using his aide, Bethany, during crunch time was no longer enough. She was running herself ragged. Her commitment was great and she, more than most, worked tirelessly to make the city she loved shine through each event.

So, tonight she planned to talk to the mayor about it. She took a deep breath. This was her time. She'd always taken care of others. It was time to step up and do something for herself. Now, with the mayor's birthday reception behind her, she could focus on her career. All she had to do was get through today, Friday the thirteenth.

Patience, Jacqueline reminded herself silently, as she

looked around the festivities for any sign of looming disaster. *It's almost over.* She glanced at her watch and noted that she had just a few more hours, and the day would be done. She could get through this. After all, she was a smart, capable, well-adjusted woman, and at twenty-nine years old, she was in complete control of all aspects of her life. Mostly.

She prided herself on being levelheaded and practical. Intellectually, rationally, logically, she knew today was just like any other day in the year. The number assigned to it was merely a label of necessary pragmatism. It was irrelevant. It was inconsequential, and she was being irrational to even give credence to the superstitions she knew all too well, but then again—

"Okay," she muttered to herself, as she looked around again, "what could possibly go wrong now?" She froze as soon as the words left her mouth. Talk about jinxing herself with bad luck on today of all days. What was she thinking?

"Jacqueline."

Her name was called. She didn't want to turn around, but she knew she had to. She recognized the boisterous voice, of course. It was the mayor of Paradise Cove, Leland Newbury. This was it, her time. She turned. He smiled as he walked toward her with his wife on his arm.

His wife, Peggy Newbury, grinned dizzily. But with a nose job, eyelid lifts, chin implants, cheek implants, lip implants, a forehead lift, Botox injections, skin peels and various other cosmetic surgeries, she couldn't do much of anything else.

As they approached, Jacqueline glanced slightly over the mayor's shoulder and saw the man she'd spotted earlier—trouble. He seemed to be following the mayor and looking directly at her. He smiled; she didn't. Then someone got his attention. He stopped and turned. Two women stepped up to him from either side. They engaged in conversation. Perhaps he wasn't following the mayor after all. She exhaled, not even realizing she had been holding her breath.

"Jacqueline, Jacqueline, Jacqueline, what can I say?"

"Mr. Mayor, happy birthday," Jacqueline said.

Leland laughed, loud and joyous. "Thank you, thank you. I came over to congratulate you. This is another fantastic event you've planned. You've outdone yourself on this one, truly outdone yourself."

"Thank you, sir," she said graciously.

"Excellent party, excellent party," Leland reiterated. "The city of Paradise Cove has been damn lucky to have you in the position of special-events manager, damn lucky."

Her heart started racing and her nerves tingled yet she began. "Thank you, sir. Speaking of job positions, I'd like to speak with you about my job and my future with the city."

"Ah, yes," Leland said, then turned and started looking around. "Now where is he?"

"Where is who, sir?" she asked.

"The state sent us a management consultant," he said nonchalantly.

"A what?" Jacqueline asked.

"A management consultant. He's going to decide about all that."

"Do you mean someone who makes changes in the guise of making generalized improvements where none are needed?" Jacqueline said, unable to keep the sarcasm from her tone.

"I wouldn't put it quite like that. He's here to help. He's been working in Phoenix for the past few weeks going through our budget and expenses. He'll be working throughout our system of operations, implementing new and improved strategy developments to optimize our operational methods."

Jacqueline was used to political double-talk. Still, her stomach quivered. She had no idea any of this was going on. She'd been too busy putting together the mayor's Scholarship Awards Program, the city's Thanksgiving Celebration and the birthday reception, to talk to him about wanting a raise previously. Now it was too late; the decision was up to someone else. Suddenly the fear of possibly losing her job shot through her. "He's here to make changes, right?"

"Yes, changes. We have to move with the times, get with the program and, yes, even tighten our belt. Budgets are being cut all over the state. City planning and management are going to take on a different look. A lot of things are going to be restructured and outsourced. But Greg will explain all that when he meets with everyone on Monday."

"Greg?"

"He has excellent credentials. Did I mention he's a lawyer and a business management specialist, too? He worked for the Justice Department, before he became a city-management consultant."

Jacqueline felt as if her brain had fried and been scrambled. She didn't know which way to turn or what to think. Then her breath caught and her nerve endings sizzled when trouble appeared again. He walked right over to stand with them. He smiled and nodded politely. She was too stunned to do anything but stand there speechless.

"Ah, here he is now," Leland said. "Jacqueline, I want you to meet Gregory Armstrong. Greg will be reporting directly to me and the city council. He'll be supervising all day-to-day operations. Right now we're in crunch time. He'll be closely monitoring your current and proposed budgets.

"Greg, this is your right-hand woman, Jacqueline Murphy. You'll be working side by side. She's a wonder with events and city planning, makes me look like I actually know what I'm doing," Leland said, then laughed riotously. "I don't know what we'd do without her. She's going to be invaluable to you."

Greg nodded. "Yes, I can definitely see that," he said, staring at her the whole time. Jacqueline looked at him blankly.

"She's a true gem. You'll see." The mayor shifted his focus again. "Jacqueline, I introduced Greg this afternoon to the staff, but you were here putting all this together. Fabulous event. Did I mention that Greg here is a lawyer, as well?"

"Yes, you did," she said, swallowing her disappointment like a bitter pill.

Greg grimaced slightly, seeing the distress in Jacqueline's eyes. She was definitely disturbed about something. "Jacqueline," he said, "it's a pleasure. I've heard wonderful things about you. I'm looking forward to working with you."

"Welcome to Paradise Cove, Gregory," she said as nicely as she could. She tried to be pleasant. After all, it wasn't his fault his main goal in life was to disrupt her future.

"Please, call me Greg. You've done an incredible job. This is a wonderful event," Greg added. She nodded.

"Indeed it is. Jacqueline is brilliant when it comes to these events. Did I tell you that she single-handedly brought two very large businesses to the area? Her city promotion ideas are exceptional. I can see you two working closely together as an unstoppable team."

"An unstoppable team. That sounds promising," Greg said.

"It is. It is. Truth be told, if it wasn't for this little lady right here, I might not have been reelected. Her ideas have put our little city on the map. People come from miles away to visit us. Tourism is soaring and we love it. Visitors are spending money and we love that, too. The 'Welcome to Paradise' campaign was her idea. We've been drawing businesses here ever since. Now that's a place where I'd really like to step up the focus. You two should get started on that. Bringing new business here means more jobs. More jobs mean happy constituents, and happy constituents means a third-term reelection. You see my point."

Everyone nodded. The mayor then began a four-minute minispeech citing the benefits of everyone working together on a common goal. He was just finding his stride when Jacqueline interrupted. "Sir, it looks like the senator is about to leave. Perhaps you should go over and speak with him before he goes."

Leland turned quickly. "Ah, yes. See what I mean, excellent ideas, carry on." With that, he cupped his wife's elbow and steered her toward the front entrance.

Greg smiled and half laughed. "You handle him very well."

"Leland's a good man and a good mayor. He's smart and cares a lot for the city and the people here. He's good for the city."

"I can certainly see that and he speaks very highly of you. I look forward to us working together very closely, Jacqueline. Perhaps we should get together this weekend and discuss..."

She nodded, then glanced over his shoulder. "Excuse me."

"Jacqueline," he said, stopping her before she walked off. "Are you okay? You seem disturbed."

"Disturbed?" she asked.

"Angry," he substituted.

"Angry?" she repeated.

"Okay, I get it. I say a word and you repeat it," he joked.

She half smiled. "Gregory, I'm not disturbed or angry. What I am is busy because I'm working. My job is to make sure everything goes as smoothly as possible."

"And you've done an exceptional job."

"Thank you." Suddenly her mouth felt dry. She licked her lips and took a deep breath. She needed to get some air. "I need to get back to work now. I have things to check on, places to be. Excuse me." She moved to breeze past him. A second later she felt him briefly touch her hand.

"Jacqueline," he said softly, stepping back and giving her more space between them. She turned back to him questioningly. "Is there anything I can do to help?" he asked.

She looked at him, seeing his sincerity. "No, but thank you for asking."

"Anytime," he said.

She nodded. "Enjoy your evening," she said quietly.

He smiled. "Thank you. You, too."

She nodded again, and then hurried off. She was just about to burst through the catering doors when she heard her name called again. She stopped.

"Hey, Jac," Bethany said, hurrying to follow. Jacqueline turned. Bethany took one look at Jacqueline's expression and shook her head. "Whoa, what happened to you? It looks like you just stuck your finger in a light socket. I guess I don't have to ask if you're having a good time and enjoying yourself."

Jacqueline turned as the mayor's young assistant walked up to her side. Bethany Allen was talented and eager to learn. She was also Jacqueline's younger sister Tasha's best friend since grade school. She was a part-time employee that the mayor had kept on after a college summer internship two years ago.

Bethany had excellent skills and would one day make a great city planner. What she didn't have was business skills. She was impatient, easily frustrated and at times lost focus, three things that didn't help in a career. What she did have was a great-uncle who was the newly reelected mayor of the city. "Sorry, hi, Bethany," Jacqueline said, calming down and composing herself. "Everything okay? Any problems?"

Bethany shook her head, and then smiled playfully as always. Like her sister, Bethany saw the world as one big, rose-colored adventure. "No problems to solve, everything's fine. Why don't you just relax and enjoy the party?"

"Yeah, maybe later," Jacqueline said.

"You say that all the time. You know, you never just let go and enjoy the moment and do something wild and unexpected, do you? Everybody's smiling, laughing and having a great time except you."

"That's because I'm working."

"Jac, you're always working. You've been working ever since I've known you. That means you've been working for over a decade. Come on, it's time to chill and have some fun. There are, like, a couple dozen single, attractive men here. Why don't you go dance with one of them? Who knows, your Prince Charming could be walking around here just waiting for you to look up and smile."

"No thanks. I've done the Prince Charming thing. It's highly overrated."

"All right, fine, so your love life is a major disaster."

Jacqueline frowned. "My love life is not a disaster."

"You got dumped via email by a pinhead jerk on Friday the thirteenth. I call that a disaster. You haven't had a date or even a one-night stand since then. I call that a major disaster."

"Can we not talk about my love life, please?"

"Why not grab a Mr. Right Now, drag him to a dark corner and kiss him until your knees buckle and your toes curl?" Bethany said excitedly.

Jacqueline chuckled. "I don't think so."

"Would you consider grabbing Mr. One Night Only, ripping his clothes off and having wild, passionate, butt-naked sex in the coatroom?" Jacqueline looked at her.

Her jaw slackened in complete amazement. "Come on, Jacqueline. I'm serious. You need to release. You're all bottled tight and wound up."

"I'm fine, Bethany."

"No, you're not. You know, one of these days, with all that pent-up energy you're gonna explode, or rather implode. Sex is an excellent stress reliever."

"Really, that's funny. Tasha said almost the exact same thing to me just the other day. Now why do I have the feeling that you and my sister have had your heads together again?"

Bethany shrugged innocently. "All I'm saying is that it's been what, over a year since you've had—"

"Bethany," Jacqueline said, quickly stopping her before she finished the sentence. She looked around in earnest, but saw no one was paying them any attention.

"I'm just saying—" Bethany began.

"Why it is that you and my sister think my private life is your personal mission is beyond me."

"I have no idea what you're talking about," she lied miserably.

"I bet you don't," Jacqueline said, as she nodded her head knowingly. The last time her sister and Bethany were on the "save Jacqueline" kick, they set her up on a blind date she knew nothing about. It was a disaster. She made them promise never to do anything like that again. Apparently she needed to have another long talk with them.

"Did I mention I heard that quickies can actually save your life?" Bethany added, discounting everything Jacqueline had just declared.

"Are you quite finished?" Jacqueline asked, frowning.

"You know my great-grandmother always said if you keep frowning, your face will freeze like that someday."

"Good thing I know better," Jacqueline responded.

"Still, you should—"

"Yes, Bethany, I know what you think I should do," Jacqueline said before Bethany could state her next outrageous suggestion.

"I was gonna say to smile. Look at all these handsome men. This is a celebration."

"No, this is work."

"Okay, okay, I tried," Bethany said, surrendering. She sighed and looked around approvingly. "Still, it looks like you did it again, another successful event." She applauded quietly.

Jacqueline smiled and nodded. "Yeah, barely, but this one was close, too close. One of these days I'm gonna open up my own business and not deal with all this added craziness."

"Oh, you say that every time," Bethany said dismissively.

"But this time I'm serious. I can't believe all the things that went wrong today—the band, the flowers, the bartenders. No, I take that back. Actually I can believe it 'cause it's Friday the thirteenth."

She knew from the first moment she opened her eyes this morning something was going to happen today; she just didn't know what. The uneasy feeling persisted all day. From past experience she knew that when it came to today, it was better to be safe than sorry.

She'd never have come out of the house if it wasn't for the birthday reception the mayor insisted on having, today of all days. His birthday was midweek, but he wanted to wait and celebrate at the end of the week. The end of the week just happened to fall on Friday the thirteenth. It was totally insane as far as she was concerned. She warned him, but he brushed it off, saying he knew she'd make everything work out. As usual, she did.

"Friday the thirteenth. Not that old superstition again." Bethany replied. "You know there's no such thing as bad luck on Friday the thirteenth. We make our own luck, good and bad."

"Yeah, right," Jacqueline said sarcastically, intent on believing differently. She knew better. She'd had too many confirmed bad-luck dramas on this day in years past not to believe otherwise.

"Well, you should ignore superstitions and open your own event consulting firm. You'd be great. I could work for you. Oh," Bethany added, obviously changing the subject, "I forgot to tell you. The city hired a management consultant. He's here tonight. He stopped by the office this afternoon."

Jacqueline took a deep ragged breath as her body stiffened. "Yes, I know. I just met him."

"I didn't get a chance to meet him yet. I left early to meet you here tonight for setup. Roger in accounting pointed him out to me a few minutes ago. Roger said he's from back east somewhere. I just got a real quick glance at him. But I can tell you, he's like supermodel gorgeous."

"I didn't notice," Jacqueline replied.

"Are you kidding me? How could you not?"

"I guess I wasn't paying attention."

"But you talked to him, right? Well, what did you think? How is he? What's he like?"

"Bethany, we really didn't get a chance to talk. The mayor just introduced us. He said hello and then complimented the success of the event," she said, while looking at her PDA. Of course she didn't tell Bethany she'd been unnerved by him when he first walked in. She'd never live it down.

"Hmm, so, I wonder where he is now," Bethany said, more to herself than to Jacqueline. She looked around the room in earnest. "I don't see him. I know he's got on a dark blue suit, white shirt and gray tie. He's got a great smile and his eyes are like bedroom sexy."

Jacqueline looked up from her smartphone at her assistant. "Wait, you got all that with just one quick glance?"

Bethany shrugged and smiled sheepishly. "It's a talent."

"Yeah, I bet," Jacqueline said suspiciously.

Bethany laughed. "Okay, okay, maybe I got a little more than just a quick glance." Jacqueline looked at her skeptically. Bethany laughed as her cheeks blushed bright red. "Okay, I admit it, I've kind of been watching him all night. But in my defense, most of the women here are doing the same thing. I swear, every time I looked over at him, another woman was trying to talk to him." She shook her head and sighed. "But who could blame them? He is too hot." She looked around again. "Wonder where he is." She paused. "Hmm, maybe he already left. And for real, if I wasn't seeing Roger, I'd seriously go after him in a minute."

"But you are, so no going after him. Roger's a good guy."

"Yeah, yeah, I know. You never let me have any fun," she pouted jokingly.

"Sure I do. As a matter of fact, here's some fun for you. It looks like the reception's breaking up. It's time for us to get back to work. You check the coatroom and make sure they have adequate coverage, then make sure the valet and cab stands are moving nicely. You can head out after that. I'll finish up here." Bethany nodded happily. "I'll be with the caterer and then the band if you need me."

"Okay, I'll call you if I need something."

"No, you have to come find me."

"What's wrong with your cell phone?"

"Working too hard. The battery charge is just about gone," Jacqueline answered.

"You want mine?" Bethany said.

"No, I'll be fine. I can use a hotel house phone if I need to call out. I don't need my cell phone any more tonight."

"You sure?" Bethany asked.

"Yes, positive," Jacqueline said. "Have a good night, drive safely. See you Monday."

"Okay," Bethany said, then turned and a second later turned again. "Do you think he's gonna make major changes?"

Jacqueline nodded. "That's why he's here."

"What if he starts laying people off?"

She shrugged. "Hopefully he won't, but we can't think about that right now."

Bethany nodded. "You know, I still think you should grab yourself a cute hottie and go buck wild."

"Maybe later tonight," Jacqueline joked. "See ya later."

"Just a thought, just a thought," Bethany said in singsong fashion, as she headed toward the coatroom.

Jacqueline shook her head at the preposterous suggestion. The last thing she needed in her life was another man. She'd had her fill with Jason. He was a backstabbing, conniving, manipulative liar. But he had taught her a very valuable lesson. From now on, her wants would always come first. As he had told her the last time she saw him, *It's never personal. It's always about business.* She took that statement to heart.

She glanced at her PDA to check the time, then quickly looked around the room. Thankfully the reception was almost over. She thought about later that night. She'd go home, shower and climb into bed alone. Alone was good, alone was safe. She didn't mind being alone.

She looked around the room again, spotting Gregory instantly. He was standing by the open patio doors talking with another man. Jacqueline watched him for a moment from across the room. Nearly everyone did at some point, she surmised. He was the kind of man you didn't overlook. But then most trouble is.

Suddenly Gregory turned and looked her way. He nodded his head in acknowledgment. She nodded her head in return. Her thoughts quickly went to what Bethany had just suggested. He smiled. She smiled, then caught herself. She turned and quickly walked away.

Across the room Greg watched Jacqueline walk away. The sexy sway of her hips tipped the side of his mouth ever so slightly. She was the last thing he needed right now.

Chapter 2

"Well, what do you think of Paradise Cove so far?"

Greg smiled. "Interesting place."

"Is that all?" Carter Gaines asked.

Greg chuckled. "Well, when I first got here, I figured I must have been in need of serious medication when I decided this was a good idea."

"Come on, man, you gotta give it a chance," Carter replied, as they walked through the stylish hotel lobby toward the exit. "You just got here this afternoon."

"Yes, and I had already been in complete culture shock just driving through the state of Arizona. How do you do it? Everything's brown and flat. This is nothing like New York or D.C."

"Exactly," Carter said, smiling.

"So far the pace is practically nonexistent. There's

no excitement, no energy, no passion and as far as nightlife—"

"There's nightlife and plenty of passion. You just have to know where to find it."

Gregory shook his head as he walked to his friend's car. His best friend, Carter, had picked him up at his place and drove them to the mayor's birthday reception. Greg chuckled to himself as he opened the passenger door. There had been one bright point this night. It took him most of the evening, but he finally got what he was looking for. After being introduced and quickly dismissed, he had watched her from across the room most of the evening. His intent wasn't to hit on her. No, his aim was pure, unadulterated personal pleasure. The simplest of joys. He just wanted to see her smile, and as he had expected, it lit up the room.

Maybe moving here wasn't such a bad idea after all. The serene slowness was literally what the doctor ordered. Sure, he had balked at first when his friend suggested it. Who wouldn't? Leaving Washington, D.C., in the midst of the most exhilarating political atmosphere in decades was a major sacrifice. But he did it; he had to. He had no choice. So, for the first six months after the Justice Department, he worked as a management consultant in Alexandria, Virginia. He found he enjoyed the extreme challenge of city politics. Then, when Carter told him that Paradise Cove was looking for a consultant, he decided to check it out.

"So, what exactly was the point of all that?" Carter asked, as he pulled away from the curb, heading back across town to drop Greg off at his new house.

"All what?" Greg asked innocently, knowing of

course his evasive tactic wouldn't work for long, if at all.

Carter laughed. "The peekaboo game you were just playing back there. She ignores you all evening, and just when she looks up and smiles, you're ready to leave. I saw you talking to her earlier. Don't tell me she's immune to the Armstrong charms." Greg looked at him dismissively. "Ha, she is." Carter laughed again. "Well, I'll be. I never thought I'd see the day when a woman looked past you."

Greg looked over at him with a confused look. "I have no idea what you're talking about."

"Come on, man, you were staring at her half the night. And you know exactly what I'm talking about. I saw your face, so don't deny it. As soon as we walked in, it was an instant attraction. You couldn't pull yourself away even if you wanted to."

"How many drinks did you have tonight?" Greg asked.

"Nah, buddy, I never drink when I'm out, you know that."

"Then you must have hit your head or something, 'cause you, my friend, are seriously delusional."

Carter chuckled again. "Yeah, I ain't the only one delusional up in here. But see, the thing I don't get is, she doesn't even appear to be your usual type. Hair pulled up tight, glasses in place, eyes cemented to her phone. Not your style, buddy. She seemed a bit too rigid and more like the girl next door."

"Rigid, yes, definitely. Still, nothing wrong with the girl next door," Greg said.

"No, not at all. But you, my friend, like the glamour party girls, quick and easy, no emotional attachments and definitely no commitments. There were plenty of them there tonight. But you spot this woman as soon as we walk in, and you can't take your eyes off of her all night."

"She was attractive," Greg said simply, as he turned to look out the side window.

"Yes, definitely, but she also looks like a keeper."

"What's a keeper?" Greg asked.

Carter slowed the car then stopped at the light. "A keeper is the kind of woman you keep around for a while, like fifty or so years. To tell you the truth, it kind of makes me wonder."

"Wonder what?" Greg asked curiously, speculating on exactly what his friend thought he knew. In all honesty, he had no idea why he couldn't take his eyes off her. As soon as he saw her, his heart jumped a beat. Then it did double time. He'd never had that reaction to anyone before.

"If you're ready to settle down," Carter said.

Greg laughed. "Again, you're delusional." But he knew Carter was right about something. She wasn't his type, but there was something about her that he just couldn't shake loose. Even now, she was still on his mind.

"This isn't D.C. and you're not litigating for the U.S. Justice Department in front of a jury. Avoidance doesn't work. You made a point of checking her out most of the evening. Then when she finally looked up, you just up and walked away. Why?"

Greg knew it was futile to continue the charades any longer. "All right, all right, I see your instinctive skills are just as sharp as ever."

"And it doesn't take instinct to see right through you.

I guess you must be losing your touch," Carter said, as the light turned green and he drove off.

This time it was Greg's turn to chuckle. Carter knew him too well. They'd known each other since childhood and their lives had intertwined for over twenty-five years. They had been elementary school adversaries, then high school rivals and finally college buddies. But this was the first time in decades they'd actually lived in the same city at the same time.

"There's no particular why," Greg said. "I was just observing my new surroundings. I have a different focus in my life now."

"I'm sure you do after the last few years you've had," Carter said seriously. "Still, why not at least talk to her?"

"She was busy, and besides, that wasn't the intent." He turned and glanced out the car window again, seeing a row of stylish storefronts.

"What was the intent?" Carter asked.

"The intent," he began, then paused to think. "The intent was to see her smile."

"Come again?" Carter said.

"Yeah, I know, it's uncharacteristic and corny, but lately I've been broadening my experiences. I'm finding the joys of appreciating the little things in life, the simple pleasures."

"A lonely impulse of delight," Carter quoted.

"William Butler Yeats," he said, smiling. Carter nodded. Greg shrugged. "Perhaps she was the first person I noticed when I walked in."

"Now that I believe. A woman in a sexy black dress, stiletto heels, slender body and also damn attractive has a way of getting a man's attention and keeping it."

"No, it wasn't that," Greg said. Carter cleared his throat as if he were choking. Greg laughed and nodded. "Okay, okay, it wasn't *just* that. What I noticed was that she didn't smile. It seemed odd. Everybody was joyful and exuberant and having a great time. But she was standing over to the side with a frown on her face as if the walls were about to tumble in on her. Seeing her smile became a simple pleasure."

Carter nodded. "I like that—a simple pleasure. But tell me, does this simple pleasure also explain why you call me and ask me to find you an investment property to purchase, and five months later you're moving in? You leave an amazing job in D.C. for a year, change careers from top federal prosecutor in the attorney general's office, with a fast-track partnership to any major law firm in the nation, to be a management consultant?"

"So what's your question?"

"The question was, should I get an order of protection or just put you in a padded room?"

Greg laughed. Ordinarily he'd be wondering himself. Carter was right; this was uncharacteristic for him. But this new turn in life was starting to grow on him. He liked the new him. "Neither. Everything's cool, really. Trust me."

Carter looked at Greg, seeing his sincerity. But while he knew that Greg wasn't lying, he also knew that he wasn't telling the whole truth. "We'll see," Carter said, only half-satisfied with his friend's explanation.

Greg knew Carter didn't completely buy his story. He also knew that he wouldn't challenge him on it at this point. The truth was, he didn't want to deal with this right now. For the past few months he'd been stressing over his life. It was now time to do something about it.

"So, are you ready for all this?"

Greg smiled, and his usual good-humored spark returned. "As ready as I'll ever be. Think they're ready for me?"

The two men looked at each other and laughed. Few were ready for Greg Armstrong. Born into the powerful Armstrong family of New York, he was the oldest son of James and Meredith Armstrong. The name drew respect in both legal and political fields. His grandfather's legacy was drawn from his father before him, and as each generation followed they added to the prestige of the Armstrong heritage. His brothers, Spencer and Cameron, had made their marks, as well.

Greg had been well on his way to adding his star to the brightly shining name. But that was before. Now he needed to take a step back and regroup. Of course, instilled with the Armstrong drive, there was no way he was going to stay dormant for long. In a few months he intended to go back to D.C. to continue his career exactly where he left off.

"I still can't believe you actually decided to come here. But I gotta warn you, this place can be addictive."

"Not for me. A few months and I'm back in Washington."

"We'll see. Paradise Cove is exactly that—paradise. It's definitely not what you're used to in New York and D.C."

"And that's exactly why I'm here," Greg assured him. "I needed to get away from all that for a while, but not forever. I just didn't realize it was going to be so—different."

"Different, but good," Carter said. Greg nodded. "You sure you're not talking about witness protection?"

"No, nothing as dramatic as that. All that other stuff is behind me and settled. Now I'm just looking for a change of scenery and a whole lot of peace and solitude."

"You'll definitely get that here," Carter said. He glanced at Greg, who suddenly looked pensive. "You sure you're okay?"

"Yeah, I'm fine. I was just thinking, three years ago I was stalked by a coworker, and after that I threw myself into my work to the detriment of everything else."

"And now…" Carter said.

"Now, I've got a clean bill of health from my doctor before coming here. My blood pressure is down, my cholesterol is on the money and my stress levels are nil. Physically, I'm back."

"But…" Carter said.

"But what?" Greg asked.

"There's something else, isn't there?"

Greg nodded his head. "Taking this year off has made me think. I was career driven for so long. I didn't realize I'd turned my back on everything else. I was missing something in my life and didn't even know it. And now that I've slowed down, I can feel the emptiness," he said. "I just don't know what that emptiness is."

Carter nodded and smiled knowingly. "You'll figure it out. In the meantime, you need to talk, I'm around. Just call." Carter held his fist out.

"Understood," Greg said, then tapped the top and bottom of his friend's fist with his own. This was their friendship; simple, honest and complete. This change was what Greg needed. Twelve months ago his life in D.C. was out of control, like his father's once was. Working eighty to ninety hours a week had gotten him on a dangerous track. His health had suffered, and his doctor told him he needed to slow down and take a break away from everything or wind up like his father, dead at forty. Two days later he had chest pains that sent him to the E.R. He'd had an anxiety attack. That scare was the epiphany that prompted him to take a leave of absence, change his lifestyle and eventually brought him here to Paradise Cove, Arizona. Hopefully, it was enough to keep him here, at least for a while.

"So, about the woman at the reception," Carter began.

"What about her?" Greg asked.

"Are you going for it?" he asked.

"She works in the mayor's office. That means we'll be working together."

Carter nodded. "So? Dude, you do know all female coworkers aren't obsessed stalkers, don't you?"

"Yes, of course, but one near-fatal attraction was enough for me. Blackmail, sexual harassment threats—she nearly ruined my life and my career."

"And what happened was three years ago."

"Yeah, so what are you saying?"

"I'm saying three years is a long time ago. You had an obsessed stalker—that was a solitary incident. After that you threw yourself into your work to the detriment of everything else, even your health. Now that you're back, maybe it's time to—"

"To what, test the waters again?"

"No, maybe it's time to stop giving up on relationships."

"I'm not giving up on relationships. Let's just say I'm taking a giant step back for clarity."

"And your coworker, the one you were watching all evening. She part of this drive-by clarity?"

Greg nodded. "Hey, I never said I wasn't tempted or attracted to her. But if she's a keeper like you say, I guess I need to keep away, since I'm just passing through."

Carter smiled. "Probably a good idea, since she blew you off anyway, right? Lucky for you there are always other options."

"A one-night stand. This isn't about sex," Greg said.

"Dude, everything is about sex. You know the rule—carpe diem, seize the day," Carter said, turning down Greg's street.

"Not this time," Greg replied.

"Yeah, right," Carter said sarcastically, "I can see the scenario right now. The two of you working late at the office. You look up at her, she looks at you, then carpe diem."

"We'll work together, yes, then I'll go home to my new place and she'll go home to hers."

"Uh-huh, right. Why do I find that so hard to believe?" Carter wondered aloud. Greg looked at him sternly. "All right, so, speaking of the new place, how's it going? Settling in okay?"

Greg chuckled. "You could say that. You wouldn't believe what my mother did. I asked her to decorate the place simply, nothing over-the-top."

Carter smiled. He knew Greg asking Meredith Armstrong, interior designer to the stars, something like that was an invitation to disaster. She only knew one way to decorate: lavishly. "I gather she didn't exactly do as expected."

"No, not exactly. She turned my place into one of her star-studded showcases. I swear, I'm afraid to touch anything."

"It can't be that bad," Carter said, parking his car on the street in front of Greg's new house.

"Come on in, see for yourself."

They got out and walked up the narrow path to Greg's duplex condo. Carter looked up to the second floor of the large structure. "Have you met your new neighbor yet?" he asked.

"No, not yet," Greg said, opening the front door. He walked inside.

Carter followed and then stopped in his tracks. His jaw dropped as he looked around and then started laughing.

"Yeah, that's exactly the reaction I had," Greg said.

Chapter 3

Jacqueline glanced at her watch as she maneuvered her car through the winding streets of downtown Paradise Cove. It was eleven twenty-one. That meant that there was just thirty-nine more minutes left in the day. She smiled with some relief. What could possibly happen to her in just thirty-nine minutes? Nothing, she surmised happily. Friday the thirteenth was almost over, and barring any unforeseen drama, she was headed home unscathed. The top was down and a warm, balmy breeze blew gently in her face. She sighed, relaxing for the first time all day. With the radio turned down low, the peaceful stillness of the evening was the perfect ending.

Her mind wandered as she thought about the evening. Everything had worked out beautifully. The mayor had had a great time—that much was obvious. And she was pretty sure everyone else did, too. She received great feedback and several notable compliments. She made a mental list of things she wanted to check on later, and then she started thinking about her conversations with Bethany.

Bethany had been worried about losing her job. She should be. They all should be. Nothing good ever came from hiring a management consultant. They could do anything in the guise of budget cuts without knowing the importance of a job or a person's worth. That meant they could easily propose layoffs and department closures. If in their opinion they didn't deem an employee worthy, that employee would be gone. She'd seen it before. Hiring a management consultant was another way of hiring an axman. Their job was to be ruthless and callous. She wondered just how ruthless Gregory Armstrong could be.

Why the mayor hired him was totally beyond her. But then, why the mayor did some of the things he did was anyone's best guess, but at times his methods of madness left her completely in the dark.

She drove through the expanding cluster of trendy stores, boutiques, galleries and restaurants in the ever-growing downtown area. Then she continued past a number of newly refurbished housing developments. Paradise Cove had certainly changed. Once a small, easily forgotten pass-through, it was now a thriving community on its way to becoming one of the more coveted upscale locations in Arizona. Several large companies had relocated nearby, bringing with them new workers and a surge of vibrant new life.

She continued through the deserted neighborhood streets, eventually turning down her street. Lined on either side were large neo-Mediterranean-styled homes, each subdivided in half, top and bottom, making two separate condo apartments. Hers was at the far end of the cul-de-sac. She lived on the top level. As she neared, she noticed that the procession of moving trucks that had been parked in front of her duplex house for the past two weeks were gone. She smiled. It appeared that at least something had gone right today. Apparently her new neighbor downstairs had finally moved in and maybe, just maybe, she could get some peace and quiet again.

She'd met the woman—her new neighbor she assumed—a few days ago while she was decorating the bottom apartment. The woman was older, in her late thirties or early forties. She seemed way too cosmopolitan to be living in Paradise Cove, but anything was possible now that the small city was expanding so quickly. She was all business with the workers, but also still pleasant enough. After a quick nod, Jacqueline dismissed her, since she didn't expect to see her much anyway. Borrowing a cup of sugar from a neighbor wasn't exactly the thing to do these days. So, she figured as long as the woman was relatively quiet, they'd get along just fine.

A feeling of satisfaction swept over her. But as she neared her house, she saw it out of the corner of her eye. In a split second, like a black flash, something darted across her path. She swerved, then slammed on the brakes. The car came to a screeching halt. The seat belt constrained her, but still she lurched forward then slammed back into her seat. Two coppery golden eyes glared at her then darted and disappeared into the darkness. Her heart slammed in her chest. "You gotta be kidding me," she said aloud. Today, of all days, a black cat had just crossed her path.

She remained completely still and cautiously looked around for signs of more hidden danger, but didn't see anything. She slowly continued driving, keeping a close, steady eye on the street in front of her. Just one house away she glanced up in the rearview mirror just in case the cat had returned. It had. It was sitting in the middle of the street, staring at her. She stopped her car and looked. It didn't move. After a while she slowly continued. Watching the rearview mirror, she turned the steering wheel and pulled into her usual driveway spot beyond the tall hedge. A split second later she looked forward. It was too late. A small, dark car was parked in her spot. She immediately hit the brakes, but she still ran right into the back of it.

She bumped her head, but the slight jarring impact wasn't bad. It was just enough to shake her up. "Oh crap." She braced her arms on the steering wheel and put her head down. This was the end of the day she had expected. She took a deep breath and paused, not noticing the two men running down the short path to her car until after they arrived.

"Are you all right?" Greg asked hurriedly.

"Open the door, but don't move her. She might be injured," Carter said quickly.

Greg grabbed the door handle and pulled just as Jacqueline pushed. The door flew open, clipping his shins. He doubled over. It was a slapstick move straight off of Saturday morning cartoons. "Sorry, are you okay?" Jacqueline said, quickly peering over the door's edge at the man's legs she'd just hit. "Sorry."

"It's okay, I'm fine," Greg said, holding the door securely away from him now.

"I'll call it in," Carter said.

"No, no, I'm not hurt, I'm fine. Don't call an ambulance. I'm fine," Jacqueline said, leaning over and grabbing at her seat belt, intent on freeing herself. She pushed to release the latch but nothing happened. She tried again. It was jammed.

"Are you sure you're all right?" Carter asked.

Jacqueline nodded. "No, yeah, I'm fine, just shaken up, that's all. I just need to get out of this thing," she said, frustrated and struggling with the safety belt. The feeling of being restrained was making her anxious. "It's stuck. I can't get this thing off. I need—"

"Here, let me help you," Greg said instantly. He knelt down, reached across her and tugged at the jammed belt. It didn't budge. He leaned in farther across her lap to get a better look at the release mechanism. Apparently when she'd fastened it, she also clipped a piece of fabric from her dress and twisted the locking portion around. Both made it difficult to release the latch with ease. Greg had to lean farther across her, turn the whole lock over and then press the release button. It worked. "I got it." Seconds later the belt released.

"Thanks, I was afraid I'd be trapped in that thing all..." she began. Then Greg turned and smiled up at her, just inches away from her face. "It's you," she said.

"Can you tell me what happened?" Carter asked.

"Umm," Jacqueline said, still staring at Greg, only vaguely hearing the question. "There was a cat," she muttered.

"Ma'am, do you know your name?" Carter asked.

"Yes, of course I know my name. It's Jacqueline," she

said, turning and looking up at the other man standing at the passenger's door asking silly questions. She recognized him, too. He had also been at the reception. She watched as the men looked at each other. They had the same expression on their faces—openmouthed astonishment. They recognized her from the reception immediately. She was the woman they had spent most of the drive talking about. And now she was here. The coincidence was uncanny.

"Ma'am, I'm Arizona State Trooper Carter Gaines," he said, as he pulled out his identification and showed her. "Are you certain you're not injured?"

Jacqueline nodded. She wasn't hurt, just completely embarrassed.

"Good, then may I see your driver's license, insurance and car registration?"

"Sure," she said, reaching for her purse. Greg, still leaning in, grabbed it from the floor where it had fallen and gave it to her then leaned back. She pulled out her wallet and handed over her ID.

Jacqueline turned back to Greg. Her heart was pounding and her stomach quivered. "What are you doing here?" she asked, looking into his penetrating eyes. They were intense and soulful and just a bit exotic, just as Bethany had said. Her stomach quivered and lurched again. Maybe she should have eaten something at the reception.

"I could ask you the same question," Greg said.

She looked away, toward her house. "I live here. This is my house."

Greg looked up at the building also. "Actually, it's my house. I live here, too. I moved in today, first floor. I guess you're my new upstairs neighbor. Now isn't that a coincidence?" He chuckled and stood up, extending his hand to help her get out of her car.

"You live here with me?" she asked, taking his hand and standing. "That's impossible."

"Not exactly with you, but close enough," he said.

"But I thought there was a woman—" she began.

"Are you sure you're okay? Your hand is shaking." She withdrew her hand instantly and held it to her head.

"Did you bump your head? You might have a slight concussion," Carter added, glancing up from the ID cards she gave him. "I can call an ambulance, or we can take you to the hospital to get you checked out."

"No, I'm fine. Really, I just thought…" Exasperated, she leaned back against the side frame of her car. She looked up at Greg. "There was a woman here a few days ago. I thought she was—"

"Ma'am, have you been drinking tonight?" Carter asked.

Jacqueline turned, hearing the absurd question. "What? No," she answered sternly.

"We saw your car swerve midway down the street then brake suddenly, and then, of course, you crashed into this car."

"No, didn't you see it? There was a cat that jumped out in front of me as I was coming down the street. It came out of nowhere. Then just now, I glanced in the rearview mirror and I saw it again. It was just sitting there in the middle of the street staring at me."

"A cat staring at you," Carter repeated. He glanced down the street, then back at her. "There's no cat in the street, ma'am." She turned around and looked down the street. The cat was gone.

"What kind of cat was it?" Greg asked.

"It was a black cat and since today is what it is, I…" Jacqueline began. She stopped, realizing now how insane she must be sounding. "You know what, never mind, it's a long, strange story. So, no, Officer, I haven't been drinking tonight," she said firmly.

"What's the big deal about today?" Carter asked.

"It's Friday the thirteenth," Greg said, as he closed her driver's side door, then leaned back against her car with ease. Carter shook his head and walked away to give them privacy. Greg looked at Jacqueline. "So, I gather you're superstitious."

"No," she said, as she glanced down the street again. "I'm not superstitious, I'm just cautious. Why ask for trouble? Is that your car?" She pointed to the black sports car parked in her space.

"Yes," Greg admitted.

"You know you're parked in the wrong space. This is my space, has been since I moved in four months ago. So actually, this whole thing is your fault."

Greg chuckled. "No, I don't think so. *You* ran into the back of my parked car, remember."

"Yes, a car that is clearly parked in the wrong space," Jacqueline argued.

"There are no clearly specified spaces here."

"I was parked here first."

"Not this evening, you weren't," he said.

"I meant I claimed this space, since I was living here first, and I believe possession is nine-tenths of the law. You, a lawyer, of all people, should appreciate that."

"I should and I do, and since I currently possess the parking space and the car that you ran into the back of, I completely agree."

She shook her head in frustration. "I should know better than to argue with a lawyer and a management consultant. You think you're always right."

He looked at her for a beat before speaking. "Is your problem with me because I'm a lawyer or because I'm a management consultant?"

"Does it matter?" she asked.

"Yes, to me it does," he said, waiting for her response.

She paused a moment to consider her reply, then smiled graciously. "Both," she said honestly.

He smiled. "I see. And for the record, we're not arguing. It's a lively debate."

Jacqueline sighed. "We're gonna have a problem, aren't we?"

"I don't see why we would."

She glared at him. "And I guess I don't see why we wouldn't. You're here to cut the city's budget. That'll have direct impact on me, my life and everything I love, including my job."

"I'm here to make this city run smoother and more efficiently. If that means there has to be sacrifices, then wouldn't you prefer they be made, rather than see the whole city suffer needlessly?"

"You make it sound almost noble."

He opened his mouth to reply, but changed his mind, knowing nothing he said would change her mind. "I'm not the enemy here, Jacqueline. I'm just doing my job. It's not personal, it's—"

"Yes, let's fall back on that old bastion, 'It's not personal, it's business.'"

"It's not and it is."

She sighed heavily. "Look, it's been a long day, so

let's just get this over with. I guess I'm on top of you," she said, then realized how it must have sounded. Greg's brow arched, then he smiled a wicked smile. "That's not how I meant it. I'm on the second floor. My condo is above yours."

"Nice to meet you, neighbor," he said. "You have a beautiful smile, Jacqueline."

"What?" She looked at him, frowning.

"I said you have a beautiful smile."

Still frowning, she shook her head as his smile brightened even more. She immediately figured she had either a nutcase or a player as a neighbor. "Thanks," she said tepidly, feeling the jitters in her stomach again. "I, um, I'd better see about the car." She took a step. Her legs wobbled and she stumbled.

"Whoa." Greg instantly moved to catch her. He quickly grabbed her around the waist, holding her in place by pressing his body beside hers and securing her against the car door. "Are you sure you're okay?" he asked softly, with added concern. "Maybe you need to sit back down." His voice was gentle and comforting.

"No, I'm fine," she said, taking a deep breath. Her chest expanded slowly. The tips of her breasts pressed tantalizingly against his arm. A few seconds later she looked up at him. Their eyes met and held, expressing something she hadn't felt in a long time. Her body tingled inside.

"Thanks, I'm okay now," she said softly.

"Are you sure?" he whispered.

She nodded, afraid to trust her voice. Suddenly the close intimacy of their physical position occurred to him. He took a step back. She stepped aside then walked to the front of her car. She looked at her car and the back of his and saw the slightly dented bumper. "Crap. Sure, of course, naturally, this would have to happen today of all days. Why am I not surprised?" There was no damage to her car, but his car's back bumper was dented and seemed to be locked under hers. "I think they're stuck together."

"So it would appear," he said, now standing behind her.

She turned. "And of course you would have to have a Jaguar."

He shrugged. "Yeah, so?"

"A black Jag," she clarified. He looked at her, still not getting her meaning. "I was trying to avoid hitting a black cat earlier, and I apparently ran right into the back of one, a black cat." He got it and started laughing. "You think that's funny, huh?"

"You gotta appreciate the irony. I guess Friday the thirteenth has a wry sense of the absurd."

"Yeah, how 'bout that," she said sarcastically, then turned back to the cars. "So, what do we do?" she asked over her shoulder.

He walked over and looked at the two cars as if to assess the situation. He stood close and pressed down firmly on the trunk of his car. It bounced up and down on its shocks a few times, then her car slipped loose. "There, good as new," he said.

"Not exactly. Your car's bumper is dented."

"I'll call a garage tomorrow. I'm sure they can take care of it quickly."

"The officer has my insurance card. We can exchange—"

"We can take care of that later. There doesn't appear

to be any major mechanical or physical damage to my car."

"Are you sure?" she asked.

"Positive," Greg said with a smile.

"Fine, then. I'll be at work tomorrow early, so if you can just get me a quote, I'll get it to my insurance company," Jacqueline said with efficiency. "And in the future, would you please park on the other side of the duplex? It would really simplify things, not to mention avoid situations like this from happening again."

He smiled, yielding. "Of course."

Carter walked back over. "Here you are, ma'am," he said, handing her back her ID and information.

"Thank you." Jacqueline took her information, then realized that she'd gotten something else back, as well. She looked at the paper. "Whoa, whoa, wait a minute. You're kidding me, right?"

"No, ma'am," he said.

She followed. "What is this supposed to be?"

"A summons," Carter said simply.

"You're giving me a summons? Why, for what reason? And how can you when you're obviously off duty driving a regular car?"

"Ma'am, you crashed your car into the back of a parked vehicle. That's called a moving violation and reckless driving. And sheriffs are never off duty."

"Correction, that's called ridiculous. I don't deserve this summons. This car doesn't even belong here. This is my spot. If anything you should give *him* the summons. Everyone on the block knows that I park here."

"I'm sorry, ma'am, rules are rules."

"I don't believe this!"

"If you have an issue with the summons you can

discuss it when you appear before the judge in traffic court. The docket number is on the back. You can call or go online and get the time of your appearance. The phone number and email address are also on the back."

"Thanks a lot," she said mockingly, then watched as the two men shook hands and returned to the car parked on the street in front of the house. She walked back to her car and looked at the damage. After a short while Carter drove off and Greg walked over.

"I'm sorry about all this," he said.

She didn't turn around. "You know what? I don't want to deal with this right now."

"You're stressed."

"Ya think?" she said sarcastically.

He chuckled at her flippancy. "Sarcasm. I would have never expected that. And here I thought you were a lost cause."

"Excuse me?" she said, turning.

"Well, you do come off tense and uptight."

"I do not."

"Actually, you do."

"I can't believe I'm actually listening to this. I am not tense and uptight. If anything, I'm organized." She turned away. Jason, her ex, had said the same thing to her. Hearing it from a different man didn't make it sound any better.

"That's not organized. That's rigid. Anyway, I'll speak with Carter and ask him to void the summons. Hopefully you won't have to go to court. We'll let the insurance companies take care of the cars."

She turned and looked at him. "Thanks," she said sincerely.

"Don't mention it. We're neighbors and coworkers now, right? It looks like you're having a bad enough day already. It's the least I could do on Friday the thirteenth."

She nodded, looking at her watch. "It's almost over," she said.

"That's right. What else could go wrong at this point?"

"Plenty," she said, then looked to where the trooper's car had been parked. "So, I assume he's a friend of yours," she said, rather than asked, as she walked back to her car and tried to close her convertible roof. The electrical mechanism didn't work, so she got out and manually tried to close it.

"Can I help you?"

"No thanks, I've got it," she said quickly.

"Yeah," he said finally. She looked up, questioning. "Carter—Trooper Gaines—and I have known each other since first grade."

"Figures," she muttered.

"You're not in a particularly great mood, are you?" he asked needlessly. She looked at him sternly. "Never mind."

"Okay, Gregory Armstrong, let's get this straight from the start. We're coworkers and neighbors, not best friends, not buds and not chums. After this evening we'll probably only see each other at work. But if by chance we do see each other around the homestead, please don't feel obligated to chat. It's okay, really. I'll understand. Good night." She started walking up the steps to her condo.

"Good night, Jacqueline Murphy," he said, then

watched as she climbed the stairs leading to her apartment. He opened his front door and went inside.

His apartment was perfect, much to his dismay. A straightforward request to his mother had turned his would-be-simple living quarters into a lavish designer abode. His mother and her staff had done an amazing job. Everything was precisely placed, down to the smallest detail. This was to be home for the next three to six months. He expected comfortable and cozy; what he got was extreme designer overload. Any other person would have been thrilled, but not him.

It was home; it was just not his home. Looking around, he knew it would take time to get used to the new place. And all he had to do was endure it for a while, then he would go back to his real home in D.C. He sat down on the sofa in the living room, opened his laptop on the coffee table and started reviewing files for his new job.

Five minutes in, he realized that he wasn't going to get anything done. His focus was shot. His thoughts kept slipping back to his new neighbor upstairs. He chuckled to himself. She was different from anyone he'd met in a long time. She apparently didn't mind saying exactly what was on her mind. Coming from D.C., he found that a welcome and refreshing change.

There, politics and prestige ruled, and lies and deception were the norm. She was certainly none of that. She was spirited, to say the least. Of course she was attractive, but in an understated way. She didn't glob on makeup or weave her hair down her back or wear acrylic nails. No, she had a simpler, more natural beauty that he found himself extremely attracted to.

That, he thought, coupled with her near-chainsaw

temper about getting a summons and his profession made her damn near toxic. There was a fire in her eyes, and each time she looked at him he felt as if he'd been ignited.

He sat back, leaned his head on the pillow and looked up at the ceiling, wondering what she was doing now. Probably getting ready for bed. The thought made an unexpected heat snake through his veins. He felt his body react. He jumped up instantly. The last thing he needed was to be thinking about a coworker that way. That was definitely taboo. He headed to his bedroom to grab a quick shower, anything to get his mind off of her.

Chapter 4

"No, no, no, this cannot be happening," Jacqueline muttered. She rummaged through her purse for the tenth time, then dumped everything out onto the outside ceramic tile floor. The four-leaf-clover key chain with the key to her front door wasn't there because she knew exactly where it was—in her bedroom on the dresser. She turned, looked at her front door and groaned miserably. Then she grabbed everything and went downstairs to her car and tried to start it.

The car clicked repeatedly but didn't start. The battery light came on and stayed on. She sighed heavily. She'd just gotten a new car battery and now it was dead. How was that possible? She slammed her palms on the steering wheel, frustrated. There was no way she'd make it to her sister's house to get her spare key. She grabbed her cell phone and dialed her sister. There was no answer. The battery was low and the cell phone beeped. She called twice more. There was still no answer. She left a message each time. Then her phone went dark and the charge light came on. "Crap."

Looking around, Jacqueline saw her neighborhood in complete darkness except for her new neighbor's home. Gregory's lights were still on. She knew she had only one choice. She needed to borrow his phone. She got out of the car, walked over to his front door, rang the bell and waited. He answered a few seconds later.

She nearly stopped breathing as her heart skipped a beat. Her eyes went directly to the obvious. His shirt was unbuttoned and open. His chest was exposed. *Good Lord.* It had been a long time since she'd seen a chest like this. Correction: she'd *never* seen a chest like this. His honey-kissed skin was perfectly smooth, and his rippled chest and flawlessly defined abs peeked through. He was magnificent. Her mouth went dry as her lips parted. *Have mercy.* A sudden lustful image eased seductively into her mind and lingered way too long.

"Hello, Jacqueline," he said, surprised to see her so soon.

"Um, hi," she said abruptly, trying to focus on the matter at hand.

"Hi," he said, smiling. "More problems with your seat belt?"

"No, not this time, actually, I locked myself out of my condo. My cell phone battery's dead, so I can't call my sister and my car isn't starting up. May I please borrow your phone?"

"Sure, come on in," he said guardedly, opening the door wider for her to enter.

A slight breeze caught the cotton material of his shirt

and made it blow open even more. She noted his broad shoulders and narrow waist instantly. The sight nearly buckled her knees. Stop it. Focus, she mentally chided herself, forcing her eyes forward as she walked inside. As soon as she did, she was amazed by what she saw. His condo was completely furnished down to the last potted plant, lit candle and throw pillow. It looked as if he'd been living there for years. "Wow."

"Do you like it?" he asked.

"Are you kidding? It's gorgeous, it's amazing. How did you do all this so fast? I expected to see a bunch of boxes all over the place."

"I have a very good decorator who took care of everything for me. All I had to do was drive out here and make myself at home."

"Oh." Jacqueline's eyes lit with understanding. "She was your decorator."

"You met her?"

"Briefly. She seemed nice. She did a great job. It looks fantastic in here. It's very sophisticated and chic."

Greg chuckled. "Yeah, it's chic, all right."

"You don't like it?" she asked.

"It's not that I don't like it, it's that this isn't exactly what I asked for."

She shrugged. "So don't pay her."

"Not exactly an option. Can I offer you something to drink, wine or coffee?"

"No thanks. I just need to borrow your phone."

"Sure," he said, as he walked over to the living room coffee table and picked up his cell phone. "Sorry, the landline isn't installed yet."

"This is fine, thank you." She took the phone, noticing it was the same type she had. She watched as he gathered files and reports from the coffee table. It was obvious he was still working on the city's financial situation. "What are you going to do?"

"About what?" he asked.

"About Paradise Cove. What are you going to do?"

"I'm still working on that."

"You must have some ideas," Jacqueline countered.

"I don't have anything substantial yet."

"Layoffs?" she asked, more worried than not.

He shook his head. "I can't say at this point."

"Can't or won't?"

"Both," he said simply. She nodded silently, knowing it was the same reply she'd given to him earlier that evening. She started dialing her sister's cell number. "Let me give you some privacy," Greg said.

He picked up his laptop and headed out of the room. Then he paused a brief moment and turned back to her. She was watching him. Her eyes seemed to be glazed over, as if she were hypnotized.

Seconds later he walked into the kitchen. He headed straight to the refrigerator and grabbed a bottle of water. As he untwisted the cap and stood in the coolness of the open refrigerator, he shook his head and thought about his new job. It wasn't popular, but it was necessary. He'd seen the files. Thanks to the last city manager, Paradise Cove was deep in financial trouble and had been for some time. The last manager had basically given the city a massive overload of borrowed money, and now it was time to pay the piper. Unfortunately he was no longer around to do it. Now Greg had to make things right, and he knew it wouldn't make him popular.

A year ago, his life was completely different. His house on the Potomac, his job with the Justice

Department; he had lived the extreme life and loved it. He lived hard, he worked hard and he played just as hard, and that included women. He dated across a wide spectrum; models, executives, lawyers, doctors and entrepreneurs. They were all lovely with plenty to offer, but he never got emotionally attached and always warned them before they got involved. Of course some didn't believe him, thinking they'd be the exception. They were wrong. He always walked away eventually.

His last girlfriend fell into that category. She was beautiful, educated and ambitious. She and her family had social connections through all segments of society. But over time she changed into someone he didn't recognize. Her calm, placid nature turned demanding and jealous. He saw the real woman. She was spoiled, needy and narcissistically possessive. She had stalked and threatened him. After her, there was a succession of equally excessive women. It became clear to him that high drama and high maintenance were no longer his style.

But there was something very different about Jacqueline. He didn't know what it was, but it was not the time to explore the possibilities. He needed to stay focused—do the job, get the city back on its feet and get back to D.C. and continue his legal career. Paradise Cove was just a pit stop on his road to recovery. And in that case he knew undoubtedly that women and work didn't mix. That lesson he learned the hard way.

In the past, both had distracted him from what was really important: his health. Working nonstop and dating high-maintenance women led him to the brink of complete exhaustion tempered with the possibilities of other health risks. He knew he couldn't do it anymore, so he stepped back, taking a break from both.

That was twelve months ago. In that time he'd learned to simplify his life. He changed his diet and learned to cook more healthy dishes. He exercised more, ate better and then cut back on his work hours. Now he felt better than he had in years. His health was great, his outlook was uplifted and his future looked bright. All he had to do was keep his focus and he'd be back in D.C.

Out of the blue he thought about Jacqueline. First, seeing her at the reception, then the accident and finding out she lived right above him, and now she was in his living room making a phone call. If he was a superstitious man, he'd wonder about all these coincidences. He took another sip of water, grabbed his laptop, closed the refrigerator door and continued to his new office area.

Just off the kitchen, the large alcove area had been converted to a perfect home office. A mahogany desk had been built in, along with a generous row of shelves and cabinets. There was also an extended credenza accommodating all of his office equipment. He walked over and sat down, placing the laptop on the desk in front of him. He opened it and began going through one of the files Leland had sent him. Reading halfway through one of the many reports, his mind started wandering.

Jacqueline. She was intriguing. She was beautiful and sexy, but in a modest way. Everything about her was understated. Even the little black dress she wore. It wasn't extravagant or flashy like some of the other women at the reception but what it did for her still had his body aching. Her hair was pulled up tight in a perfect twist, giving her neckline a sweeping elegance. But it was the glasses that had interested him. They seemed to work more as a barrier than a necessity. He allowed his thoughts to wonder at the sweet possibilities of taking those glasses off. Soon he felt his body's arousal and caught himself. He had no intention of acting on his musings, so he pushed away the thoughts and went back to reading the mayor's report.

Jacqueline had turned to watch Greg leave the living room. He walked with confidence, in a smooth, elegant motion, reminiscent of a proud warrior. An easy smile tipped her full lips. His body was perfect; broad shoulders, slim waist, flat, firm stomach and so sexy, long, slightly bowed legs. Instantly she remembered their brief interlude, him steadying her against the car. She still felt the power of that innocent intimacy—his body pressed to hers felt right. His embrace was strong, firm and gentle. Still musing and staring, she caught herself, but not before Greg spotted her.

"Jacqueline, anything I can do?" he had asked softly before leaving the living room.

Startled, she swallowed hard. How could she have been so obvious? He'd caught her staring. "Mmm-hmm, no, I'm okay," she muttered nonsensically, then nodded sheepishly. He nodded and turned. She quickly sat down. A few seconds later she turned again. This time he had gone from the room. She physically relaxed and dialed her sister's cell phone. She collapsed back into the comfortable sofa and took a deep breath, exhaling slowly and deliberately. "Good Lord," she whispered to herself, "what is wrong with me?" It only took a few seconds for the answer to pop up. Bethany was right, it had been too long. She was lonely, and having a man like Gregory around was a desperate reminder of what she didn't have in her life.

It had been close to a year, and now she was feeling the loneliness and the desire more than ever. "Come on, come on," Jacqueline muttered, as her sister's phone rang a third time. She needed to get out of there fast before she did or said something desperate.

It had been a long time since Jason, her ex-boyfriend. He was smart, ambitious—and a total jerk. They'd been together for two years. In the beginning he was everything any woman could ask, then in time he changed. He had promised her the world and that he'd be with her forever. He lied. As soon as a better job offer came along, he left for Phoenix and never looked back. He did, however, thank her for being so supportive over the years. She still couldn't believe he wrote the "supportive" part.

The cell phone rang two more times. "Come on, Tasha, come on. Pick up the phone, answer." She didn't. Jacqueline called her sister's home number. It rang three times then went to the answering machine. She left another message then tried her cell again. She pressed the end button on the cell phone and looked around for her host. "Gregory," she called out.

"I'm in here," he answered.

She found him sitting in a large alcove near the kitchen with his laptop on a beautiful built-in desk. It was his office area, and it was perfectly situated, closed off and still easily accessible. He looked up as soon as she entered. He'd buttoned his shirt. "Everything okay?" he asked.

"Actually, no. My sister isn't answering her cell phone

or her house phone. Do you have a phone book? I need to call a cab."

"A phone book, uh, sure." He stood and looked around the office, then frowned as he opened a few drawers and cabinets. "You know what? I truthfully have no idea where my phone book would be, or if I even have one yet."

"That's okay, thanks anyway. I'll go next door and ask."

"Jacqueline, it's after midnight."

She glanced at her watch; he was right. Friday the thirteenth was officially over.

"I'm sure the last thing you want to do is wander around in the middle of the night asking neighbors for a phone book. If you want to go to your sister's house, I'll drive you."

"No, I couldn't impose like that. I'm sure you have things to do. You're working."

"It's nothing that can't wait and it's no imposition. Come on." They went outside and headed to his car.

"My car is blocking you in and it's dead."

"Dead?"

"The battery light came on and stayed."

"Do you need a jump?"

"No, I'll call the garage tomorrow. Just a ride would be fine."

"Okay, I'm sure driving on the lawn this one time won't cause too much damage." She nodded, seeing no other way. "Did you consider that your sister may not be home?"

"She probably isn't."

"So, I guess you have a key to her place, right?"

"Yes, of course," Jacqueline said, then a few seconds

later she stopped walking. "It's on the same key chain with my front door key, which is on the dresser in my bedroom. I separated the car key from the other keys when I took my car to the repair shop yesterday. I got busy and didn't reconnect them again." She shook her head. "I can't believe this. I'm stuck. No keys. No car. No nothing." She looked around into the darkness, completely exasperated.

"You don't have a place to stay tonight," he said.

She thought a moment. "Yeah, I do. I'll stay in my car."

"You can't sleep in your car."

"People do it all the time."

"I can't let you sleep in your car. That's ridiculous."

"I'll be fine."

"No, look, there's a simple solution."

She turned. "What is it?"

Greg paused. He couldn't believe he was about to make this offer but he couldn't knowingly have her sleeping outside when he had an extra room in his place. "Spend the night with me," he said hesitantly.

"Excuse me?" she said, surprised by his offer.

"Spend the night with me. I have plenty of room."

"Aah, no, not an option, not even close," she said.

"Why not?" he asked. "The alternative is your car."

"Because I don't even know you, that's why not."

"True, and of course I don't know you either. But still, I'm willing to open my home to you for the night. So unless you have more family in the area or friends you'd like to wake up at this time of night, I'll be happy to drive you wherever you'd like to go. But it's crazy to sleep in a car when I have a second bedroom available."

"There's a hotel not too far. I'd appreciate a ride."

"Jacqueline."

"A ride, please," she said. "Thank you."

"Is that really necessary?" Greg saw her waffling. "Look, we're neighbors and coworkers. Right now, know that I'm a gentleman and I can't have you walking the streets in the middle of the night looking for a place to sleep. My condo has two completely furnished bedrooms. It makes sense."

She looked at him trying to judge his character before deciding. It was late, she was tired and she had an early day tomorrow. The last thing she wanted to do was sleep in her car. "Okay, thank you. I really appreciate this."

"You're welcome. Now come on. It's been a long day. Let's get to bed." As soon as he said the words, he stopped and looked at her. Jacqueline looked at him suspiciously. "That's not how I meant that."

She nodded then smiled. "I know." They walked back to his condo and went inside.

Chapter 5

Greg led the way. Jacqueline followed. Her eyes roamed freely as they passed through the living room to the dining room. She looked around admiringly, and then settled on him. He walked majestically, with each stride confirming his confidence. Broad shoulders, narrow waist, tight, perfect rear. She mentally checked off each attribute, then caught herself and quickly stopped, glancing instead at her surroundings. Everything was perfectly placed, including the fresh flowers on the dining room side table. "Your place is really beautiful," she said, her voice weaker than usual.

"Thank you," he said.

She watched him again, broad shoulders, narrow waist, tight...she stopped and cleared her throat to refocus. "So you said before that you drove here. From where?"

"Phoenix, by way of the Washington, D.C., area," Greg answered.

She nodded. "Is that where you're from, D.C.?" she asked, as they continued toward the bedrooms in the back of the condo.

"Actually I grew up in New York. Most of my family still lives there. What about you?"

She smiled readily with pride. "I was born and raised right here in Arizona. I even went to college here."

"A hometown girl. I guess you know the area very well," he said, as they walked down the hall and stopped at the second door.

"Yeah, I do," she said.

"That's good to know."

Greg opened the door and showed her the extra bedroom with its own adjoining bathroom. Jacqueline walked in and looked around. It was just as beautiful as the rest of the condo. "Wow," she said, "this is beautiful." She circled the room, first walking to the window and drapes, then over to the large antique armoire. Afterward, she moved to the queen-size sleigh bed against the far wall. She ran her hand over the matching damask. It was soft and luxurious.

He stood staring, watching her intently and seeing new aspects of her beauty. His eyes were riveted to her every move. She wasn't supermodel glamorous like some of the women he'd known in New York and D.C., but she was still beautiful, with a sweet, classic styling that was easy and uncomplicated. She picked up one of the many silk throw pillows from the bed and held it tight then turned to Greg. "It's perfect."

"Good," he said, smiling. "I'm glad you like it."

"Who wouldn't?" she said. "You know, it's so hard

to believe we live under the same roof. Your place is so different from mine. I have a second bedroom too, but it seems a lot smaller than this room."

"I think my designer had a few walls moved around."

"Can she do that? I mean what about the owner or the building codes?" Jacqueline asked.

"Believe me, Meredith's a perfectionist and a stickler for rules, regulations and details. She wouldn't have done it if it wasn't perfectly up to code. And trust me—the owner had no problem letting her do what she needed to do. Meredith can be very persistent when she wants to be."

"From what I noticed, she was all business and extremely focused on the job. I liked her style."

"I'll make sure to tell her that."

"Sounds like you know her pretty well."

"I do. You could say I've known her all my life."

Jacqueline paused. "That sounds very mysterious."

"Not at all," he assured her.

"Does she live here with you, too?" she asked, knowing that she shouldn't have. But the idea of Meredith as a cougar didn't seem too far-fetched. "I'm sorry, that was too personal," she added.

"Yes, it was," he said, smiling, knowing her intent. "But no, she doesn't live here with me. Although I'm sure she'll be stopping by on occasion."

Jacqueline nodded, not quite getting his full meaning. She decided not to pry further. "Well, thanks again. I really appreciate this. I'll be up and out early tomorrow morning."

"No rush, take your time," he said. His expression

changed. His eyes shone with added vivacity. They paused, looking at each other a few seconds.

"So, I guess this is good night," she finally said quietly.

He nodded. "Let me know if you need anything else."

"No, I won't. This is perfect. I'm sure I'll be fine. Good night," she said softly. He closed the door behind him.

Greg went to the kitchen to his office area in the alcove. His laptop was already open, but the screen was dark. He pressed the refresh button and the screen illuminated almost instantly. He sat down and took a deep breath. The sweet lingering scent of Jacqueline's perfume filled his lungs. It was obvious that his self-imposed refrain from intimacy was definitely taking a hit tonight.

He shook his head woefully. Maybe Carter was right. It's always about sex, or in his case the lack thereof. It had been five months and counting. His body tensed at the mere thought. Having Jacqueline in his home reminded him exactly what he'd given up.

As soon as Greg left, Jacqueline sighed heavily, and then dropped down on the side of the bed. Her body immediately sank farther into the deep memory-foam mattress. She lay back and felt the padding surround her and yield to the exact contours of her body. She must be insane. She was actually in a stranger's home, lying on his bed, with him in the next room. She sat up and looked at the door. Maybe she should lock it. She stood up to secure it, just as her purse slipped off the side of the bed. It fell open and her cell phone came out, reminding her she needed to try her sister again. She picked it up and pressed a button. The screen remained black. She needed a charge.

She opened the bedroom door and stepped into the hall. "Gregory," she called out softly, as she looked down the hallway toward what she knew was the master bedroom. He answered from the front of the condo, thankfully. She turned, followed his voice. She found him sitting in the office area again. "Hi, sorry to disturb you…"

"You're not disturbing me, Jacqueline," he quickly said, "and please call me Greg."

She nodded. "I was wondering if you had an extra charger for my phone." She held it up.

"Sure," he said, eyeing the cell phone in her hand. "It looks as if we have the exact same model. Just place it here on the pad, it should charge with no problem."

"Thanks," she said, placing her cell on the pad next to his. "So I guess this is good night again." He nodded. She turned to leave then paused midway down the hall, looking down at her dress. It was stylish, formfitting, nearly backless and way too expensive. It was perfect for a reception, not so perfect for sleepwear. The idea of sleeping in her one and only extravagance didn't appeal to her. Neither did sleeping in just her underwear and nothing else. She turned back.

"Ah, Gregory, one more thing, do you have something I could sleep in?" She looked down at her black cocktail dress. "This isn't exactly sleeping attire."

"Sure, come on. I'll find something for you," he said, standing. They walked down the hall to the master bedroom. The door was already slightly open. He crossed the large room to the dresser and pulled out a couple of T-shirts. He turned around, seeing her still standing in the doorway staring at his king-size bed. With throw pillows, shams and matching damask, it was elaborately made and looked like a showroom centerpiece. He watched as her eyes slowly roamed over the rest of the bedroom.

"Wow, she really is very talented," she said, overwhelmingly impressed.

"Meredith. Yes, she is. Come on in, have a look around," he offered.

"No, that's okay," she said shyly, staying put.

"Don't tell me you're afraid," he tempted teasingly, as he casually leaned back against the dresser. She didn't respond. He stood tensely. "Jacqueline, I assure you I would never—"

"No, no, I'm not afraid," she said truthfully, interrupting him, "and I do trust that you're a gentleman." She looked at him, assuring her trust.

He nodded. "Then what is it?" he asked softly.

She shook her head and sighed heavily. "I just don't know what to make of this night. It hasn't exactly turned out as I expected, as I planned." The exasperation in her voice was evident.

He smiled, knowing exactly what she meant. "Rumor has it that life rarely goes according to plan. I learned that the hard way. But I bet you plan every second of your day, don't you?" Her eyes lit up instantly. He knew he was right.

"Well, that is what I do for a living. So, what's wrong with planning?" she asked.

"Nothing. It just makes life a bit predictable, don't you think?"

"That's funny coming from you. Isn't that what you do too? Plan, strategize about people?"

"No, I research, investigate and improve management programs. I see waste and eliminate it."

"One person's waste is another person's job," Jacqueline countered.

"There are other jobs."

"In this economy? Please," she said sarcastically. "People can look for months, even years, before finding something else. What happens to their mortgage, electricity, food, family?"

"That's not my—"

"Yeah, not your concern, I know that. Look all I'm saying, asking, is that you consider the human factor when you make your recommendations."

"What I was going to say is that's not my job. I don't arbitrarily hatchet and ax people. I'm not some modern-day, guillotine-happy executioner." The grimace on her face instantly turned into a smirk then slowly to repressed laughter. Apparently his remark humored her. "You find that funny?"

"Sorry, the mental picture popped into my head."

"I'm afraid to ask."

"Don't."

He smiled, too. There was a calm moment between them, as it seemed each stepped back to their respective corners. "Jacqueline, I'm not the enemy here. I simply clean up other people's overzealous chaos and get them back on track. Yes, sometimes the human factor takes a hit. But the sustaining good of the organization is my first and only concern."

She nodded, not necessarily agreeing but understanding. "And for the record, there's nothing wrong with planning and being predictable. Predictable is comforting and reassuring. It's stable. It's a good quality," she said defensively, knowing both her parents were anything but responsible. Her childhood was erratic, unpredictable and in some cases sheer chaos. When she was old enough, she took control. Since then, she had never looked back.

"You're right, it is. But sometimes you gotta let it go," he said. She shook her head no. "Come on, I bet somewhere in your past you were carefree, laid-back and totally spontaneous."

"Me? No, sorry, you'd lose that bet."

"Come on, haven't you ever just relaxed and enjoyed the moment or done something completely out of character?"

"No, never," she said adamantly.

"Have you ever wanted to?" he said, tempting her.

A slow, sly smile tugged at her full lips. "Sure, I guess maybe I've thought about it before."

"Okay, then right now, this moment. Do something completely out of character and spontaneous."

"What? No, I can't."

"Yes, you can," he assured her. "Whatever you want to do, just do it."

She bit at her lower lip as she considered his suggestion. It was tempting. But doing something spontaneous wasn't her. She was the planner, forever safe and steady. She was the dependable one. She was always in control, always responsible and reliable. Still… "Like what?" she asked.

His lips curved knowingly. He knew she'd made up her mind. "That's up to you. Don't think about it, just do it," he instructed.

Jacqueline felt the intensity of his eyes. His gentle encouragement was enticing her, and she felt herself yielding. A rush of adrenaline surged through her veins. He was challenging her and she was tempted. For the first time in a long time she felt nervous and excited. She was in complete control, but yet had no idea what she was doing. She liked the feeling. She walked over to stand in front of him, and then on a whim, she reached up and touched his face softly. He tensed. She tiptoed up to kiss his cheek. "Thank you for tonight."

They stood in silence. Then, looking at him, a searing blaze swept over her. Her body ached to be held. Seconds later she wrapped her arms around his neck and kissed him desperately. He grabbed her waist and drew her body closer, pressing his back against the dresser. The kiss deepened to something she hadn't expected. Passion, desire and need erupted for both of them. A second, three minutes, an hour, she had no idea how much time had elapsed. All she knew was that this was real, and either she would surrender completely or get out of there fast. She leaned away and took a step back.

She looked into his piercing eyes. "Oh my God, we can't do this. What am I doing here with you?" She turned to walk away.

He captured her hand. She looked back. "This," he answered, and instantly she was back in his embrace. All caution flew to the wind. He kissed her quickly, then again. Each time he paused for her reaction. The third kiss came. It was longer, languishing deep in passion and promise. When it ended they looked into each other's eyes. It was more than either could stand. The fourth kiss exploded and then there was more, so much more.

There was a tangle of arms and bodies pressed together as one.

Reality had been eclipsed by the fantasy of his embrace. Jacqueline had never been so completely consumed by a kiss. Her response was instantaneous. She moaned deep in her throat. He gripped her tighter, pressing her close. He wanted her to know his arousal. She did and knowing this power over him was exhilarating. All she had to do was…yield.

Suddenly she leaned back. He instantly released his hold. She placed her hand on his large chest as if to pause the moment. She took a deep, ragged breath. "I can't," she whispered breathlessly, softly moaning her pleasure and regretting the words even as they slipped from her lips. "This isn't me." She kept her head down. There was no way she could look into his eyes. If she did she knew she'd be lost, wanting more than just a second and third helping. "I can't," she repeated, more to herself than to him. He leaned down and picked up the T-shirts from the floor. She slipped one from his hands, stepped aside and walked out as steady as she could.

She hurried back to the bedroom and closed the door behind her. Her legs wobbled and her body shook. She had no idea what she would have done had he called out to her. Thank God he didn't. There was nothing to say after that display. It was clearly a case of a lapse in judgment and momentary insanity.

Greg shook his head in disbelief. What was wrong with him? What was he doing? Whatever just happened, he needed to make sure didn't happen again. He followed Jacqueline, then saw her bedroom door close. He raised his hand to knock and apologize, but then stopped. Maybe this wasn't the time. They both needed to cool off. He still couldn't believe what came over him. It had been a while, sure, but he'd never felt passion sweep over him like that. And he intended for it never to happen again. Jacqueline was a coworker, and that made her taboo. He had vowed to himself to never get involved with another coworker, and he intended to keep that promise.

He continued to the office alcove and grabbed his water and laptop, then headed back to his bedroom. He sat down on the comfortable sofa and opened a file. He scanned it quickly then stopped and looked across the room. Just moments ago he was kissing his neighbor and coworker there. His body was still roused. But he could control his desire; when a woman said no, that was it as far as he was concerned. But he saw the wavering in her eyes. In that instant she wanted him as much as he wanted her. But she held tight. He believed her when she said this wasn't her. He liked that, too.

"So much for carpe diem," he said, then went back to work.

Chapter 6

Momentary insanity.

He wasn't that special, Jacqueline mentally declared. So what if he had bedroom eyes that had turned her legs to rubber? So what if when he said her name, her heart thundered in her chest? So what if when he looked at her, she wanted to strip off every piece of clothing and make love to him right there?

He was the enemy—well, maybe not the enemy, but he could certainly affect her life, and that made him dangerous. Kissing him was insanity. Kissing him again would put her squarely in the "trading intimacy for favors" category. That wasn't her, and in all honesty it didn't appear to be him, either. He seemed just as surprised by the sudden moment of passion as she was. But it wouldn't happen again, of that she was certain.

She tossed and turned as thoughts raced. It wasn't that

she was in her new coworker's bed, in his condo, with him right in the next room. No, it was that she'd kissed him and she liked it. She liked it—her body was still on fire and aching for more—she really liked it. What was she thinking?

Kissing men she didn't know, complete strangers, was totally out of character for her. Jacqueline didn't often date and never slept around in the guise of having fun or being free. That was her father's style, not hers. And she was nothing like her father.

She could still feel his arms as they wrapped around her tightly, his hands spread wide, pressing her against the hardness she most definitely felt. "Stop it," she told herself, then rolled over in bed, grabbed a pillow and placed it over her head.

This was all Bethany's fault. If Bethany hadn't suggested she do something wild and spontaneous, she never would have thought about kissing Gregory, and in the middle of his bedroom, no less. Knees buckling and toes curling, that's what Bethany had said. Then rip his clothes off and have wild, passionate, butt-naked sex. As it happened, Jacqueline came close, way too close.

She touched her fingers to her lips. The kiss had been hours earlier, but she could still feel the strong, sensuous pressure of his lips on hers. She closed her eyes and took a deep breath. Then she sat up, turned and punched the pillow down in frustration. Unfortunately, it didn't help much. This was going to be a very long, sleepless night.

Wondering what it would be like to make love to him, her body finally relaxed into comfort. Her wondering turned to fantasy, then to dreams, as she finally fell asleep.

She was laying back on something hard and cold, but she didn't really feel it. Her body was hot. It was on fire. She was looking up at the night sky. A trillion stars sparkled and shone down on her. Her breathing was ragged and came in short, uneven gasps. Her heart raced and every nerve in her body tingled. Somebody was there with her. He was kissing her, touching her, caressing her, feeling her. He was everywhere, all over her body, all at the same time. She moaned with pleasure because now it was different. He was doing something else to her. She closed her eyes and gasped loud and long. Her breathing became shallow and irregular, increased to urgency.

She felt her body weaken. A dizzying, floating sensation came over her. The man, the stranger, was taking her to places she'd never been before. His mouth was hot, licking his way back down, then up her body; her thighs, her hips, her stomach, her breasts, then her neck to her lips. Kissing her set her body on fire all over again. Then he was there, and she felt the hardness of his body and his penis pressing on top of her. He throbbed with want. She shuddered with need. Her legs parted to him. She surrendered, giving him all he demanded.

She reached her arms out wide, feeling hard, unyielding steel beneath her body as the same unyielding hardness entered her. She screamed her sudden pleasure as her body shook. He had filled her, and she savored the long, hard thickness inside. Gasping, her body went still as he slowly moved in and out. He reached beneath and lifted her hips to deepen the penetration. Long, luscious strokes that lasted a lifetime dipped into her body. Over and over again she felt him fill her. He leaned up higher, touching and stroking her there. Her body nearly seized.

He knew exactly how to bring her pleasure. She trembled in anticipation, wanting more. But he didn't give it all at once. No, the drawn-out ecstasy of her pleasure went on and on. Then he'd hit that spot and make her scream all over again.

The swirling swell of his torturous delight ebbed her closer and closer to that pinnacle she knew was coming. Holding back was out of the question. She was helpless. He knew her body too well by now. So she yielded, not wanting to prolong her imminent release any further. She needed to hold on to some semblance of control. But he wanted more from her. He took more, draining her body. He wanted all of her now and she, helpless, surrendered everything.

Her breath caught quickly. She arched her back upward. His mouth instantly captured a pebbled nipple and suckled, drawing her into his hot mouth. She screamed her pleasure, knowing she was seconds away. In tumultuous disorder the maelstrom was coming and she writhed and shook. One instant became a lifetime. She neared her climax. Coming, coming, coming...

She awoke and sat straight up, panting hard and looking around. It was still dark and she was alone. It was just a dream. But it felt so real, too real. She lay back down. It was going to be a very, very long night. She closed her eyes thinking about the dream. A few minutes later she fell back asleep and dreams came once more.

Just before dawn Jacqueline woke up, after three hours' sleep. She dressed quickly, then stepped out into the hall. Gregory's bedroom door was closed, so she went back to the office area to get her phone. There was a dimly illuminated night light on the desk. She grabbed her cell and hit Redial.

Tasha picked up on the third ring. "Hello?"

"Hey, it's me," she whispered.

"Jacqueline?"

"Of course, who else would it be?"

"I was gonna call you back in a little bit. What's up? How was the Friday-the-thirteenth birthday reception last night?" she asked encouragingly.

"It was fine and thankfully behind me."

"Cool. So what's up? You left me, like, a hundred messages."

"Where were you?" Jacqueline asked quietly.

"Sin City."

Jacqueline's heart jumped and her mind raced. Already married and divorced by the age of twenty-four, her younger sister, Tasha, was the romance equivalent of a head-on collision. She dutifully fell in love regularly and just as dutifully got her heart broken. Her absolute devotion to lost causes and her resilience to move on to the next disaster was astounding. The one good thing was that she'd married a very wealthy guy without a prenuptial agreement. The one bad thing was that she divorced him a month later to prove she truly loved him. Able to get an obscene alimony from him, she passed on principle. Unfortunately, he moved on.

"Las Vegas? Are you kidding me? Please, please, please don't tell me you ran off to Vegas and got married again."

"Don't be so melodramatic. And because I'm in such a good mood, I'm gonna ignore that remark. And no, to answer your very rude question, nothing as drastic as that. I was in Vegas visiting a friend."

Jacqueline physically relaxed, not realizing she'd been holding her breath. "Sorry. So, where are you now?"

"I'm on my way home."

"Can you stop by my place? I locked myself out last night."

She chuckled. "You, Ms. Plan Everything? How in the world did you lock yourself out?"

"It was Friday the thirteenth. Need I say more?"

"Why not just go to my place?"

"The car won't start and your front door key is with mine."

Tasha laughed. "I swear—you and Friday the thirteenth. Does anything ever go right for you on that day?"

Jacqueline decided not to answer. "Can you stop by?"

"Yeah, sure, I should be there in about half an hour or so. So where'd you sleep, in the car?"

"No, I'll tell you later. It's a long story. I'll see you in a half an hour."

Jacqueline went back into the bedroom, made the bed and made sure the room was exactly as she found it. She grabbed her purse and headed to the living room to wait for her sister. There was a low light still on, so she sat by the front window and watched for any sign of her sister's headlights. Her thoughts started wandering to the man asleep in the next room.

Gregory was handsome and sexy, and he had to be affluent enough to afford a designer like Meredith. Everything about Meredith screamed money and power: her looks, her clothes, even her attitude. You just don't put a down payment on her services and ask about a layaway plan.

She looked around and shook her head in awe. Her place was nice but this was showroom spectacular. It was rugged, masculine and refined all at the same time, with just a touch of elegance. It suited him. From what little she knew of Gregory, he seemed to be all those things.

Her stomach quivered as she remembered the sight of him opening the door earlier with his shirt unbuttoned. Good Lord, the man had a body a woman could fantasize about all night. Then she remembered the dream. Every touch, every caress, every detail came to life. Her body tingled. There was no need to go further. The dream was enough to start her up all over again.

Needing a distraction, she looked back through the living room and dining room to the soft, illuminating glow coming from the office desk just beyond the kitchen. He was a lawyer in Washington, D.C. He never said why he came here, of all places. Paradise Cove wasn't exactly on the beaten track. It was as far away from big-city politics as you could get. Up until a few years ago, most people moved away from the area, not to it.

Then a few large companies moved nearby and now there was a near explosion of possibilities. Paradise Cove was finally on the map as one of the last great places to live. Smaller companies, stores, boutiques, galleries all started coming. They brought an influx of presumption, attitude and entitlement. Those who knew the small, quietly reserved city were all of a sudden displaced for the sake of capitalism and free enterprise. Certainly the new energy revived the city of Paradise Cove but it came at the expense of everyone who had faithfully called it home for so many years.

Without thinking, she touched her lips again. The kiss she and Gregory shared suddenly felt as if it had just happened. She had intended to shock him with her spontaneity, but she was the one that was surprised. Her body was still reeling and feeling the ravages of just a few moments with him. She closed her eyes, thinking about her bold march over to him, touching his face, leaning in, kissing him. After that everything went sideways.

The simple, quick thank-you kiss she expected had turned into an oral seduction. She melted into his arms as if she'd been born to. And he held her with purpose and pursuit. Their mouths connected over and over and over again, as their tongues danced and mated lasciviously. When they stopped, they gazed into each other's eyes. After that, everything seemed to explode. A raging flood of need, desire and want enveloped her.

The sensation of feeling his body harden against her stomach had spurred her boldness. She pressed her hips closer as the kisses deepened, each more sensuous and erotic than the last. Their hunger was suddenly insatiable. Her body throbbed, wanting more. He'd turned, reversing positions, pressing her body back against the dresser.

Then his hand held the back of her head as his other hand slid between their bodies. He caressed her neck, her shoulder and arm, then her breasts. He went down, burying his face in her neck, between her breasts and against her stomach. He eased himself lower, touching and feeling the softness of her body everywhere. She closed her eyes, reeling with the sensuous sensation. He massaged her soft mound, tantalizing her nipples to harden against her silky dress. She was sure she had stopped breathing.

"Enough," she muttered to herself in the darkness of the empty room, feeling her body tingle all over again. "Just stop thinking about him." She looked around, feeling self-conscious. There was no one around; still she felt silly. What was going on with her?

She dug through her purse and found her cell phone. She pressed a key and illuminated the time display. It was five-fifteen in the morning. She stood and looked out the window. There was still no sign of her sister. She sat back down, tucking her feet beneath her. She laid her head back and closed her eyes. A few minutes later she was asleep again.

Chapter 7

The double beeping sound of a car alarm's activation made her jump. She tossed off the throw covering her and hurried to the window. Her sister's car was parked in front of the building. She went to the front door, opened it and peeked outside. There was no one there, but she heard footsteps. She peeked out farther, seeing her sister heading up to her condo. "Tasha," Jacqueline whispered.

Her sister stopped and turned midway up the stairs. She smiled. "Hey, Jac, what are you doing in there? Whose condo is that?"

"Shh," Jacqueline said. "I'll be right there." She went back inside, grabbed her purse and cell phone, then noticed the throw that had covered her on the floor. She picked it up, folded it, then realized she hadn't covered herself. It must have been Gregory. She turned around.

He wasn't there, but he must have been there earlier, after she nodded off. Her stomach quivered, knowing he had watched her sleep. She stepped out of Gregory's condo, closed and latched the door quietly behind her. "Let's go."

"You have a new neighbor?" Tasha asked.

Jacqueline nodded. They went up to her place. Tasha opened the door. As soon as Jacqueline walked in, she felt some semblance of control return. She was back in her condo and all was well.

"So what happened last night?" Tasha asked.

"What do you mean?" she asked quickly, defensively.

Tasha looked at her questioningly. "I mean the mayor's birthday reception. What do you mean?" she asked jokingly, knowing her sister had the social life of a sleeping pill.

"Nothing."

"What is up with you? You're acting really weird."

"I'm fine, just tired."

"So, how was it?"

"How was what?" she asked unable to keep an innocent expression.

"Okay, what's going on with you? I'm talking about the mayor's reception last night."

"Oh, that. It was fine."

"'Oh, that'?" Tasha repeated, mimicking her sister. "Since when do you refer to a city event as 'oh, that'?"

"It was fine. I'm just tired. I didn't get much sleep."

"So who's the new downstairs neighbor?"

"I don't know. Somebody from D.C.," Jacqueline said, yawning.

"You're just full of information this morning, aren't you?" Tasha said. "You stayed at 'somebody's' place all night and you don't even know them. That's seriously not you. You know what? I like it," Tasha said cheerfully.

"Don't get your hopes up. I was desperate. My car died again and my cell needed charging. I had no place else to go, and he offered me his guest bedroom."

"He? His?" Tasha repeated. "So that somebody is a guy."

"Never mind," Jacqueline said.

"Girl, your cell phone isn't the only thing that needs charging. So, is he nice?"

"He's all right, I guess."

"Young? Single?"

"Yes, and I don't know. It's none of my business." Tasha nodded. "Attractive?"

"Yes, very attractive," she said painfully.

"So, are you going for it?"

"Going for what?" Jacqueline asked. She knew exactly what her sister was asking, but she stalled for time to get the image of him standing in the doorway with his open shirt out of her mind.

"Him, that's what. Are you going for him?"

"No, definitely not. He's a management consultant hired by the city. He's here to cut the budget—that means possible layoffs. Then there's the woman I told you about. The one I thought lived downstairs. Apparently she was the decorator, but I have a feeling she was more than that."

"Is she there now?"

"No."

"So then, go get him."

"Tasha, you make it sound like I should be some kind of manhunter and he's the prey."

"That's exactly it. Bethany told me how you were all closed off last night at the reception. She said there were men everywhere and you were single-focused on work. Jac, this 'all business, no pleasure' thing isn't right. Just because Jason dumped you with that stupid 'I need to put my career first' line doesn't mean it's right for you, too."

"He was right. I do need to put my career first just like he did. I spent two years waiting, hoping and praying for him to step up. When he did, it was on my heart, then out the door. I was hurt, but not anymore. Jason's walking out and leaving turned out to be the best thing for me."

"Now that I agree with one hundred percent. He didn't deserve you but don't shut every man out just because of him."

"I'm not taking romance advice from you."

"When's the last time a man even called you not related to business? Speaking of which, when'd you get the new cell phone number?"

"What new cell-phone number?"

"The one you called me from last night and then again this morning. It's not your phone number. That one has a two-zero-two area code."

"No, it doesn't," she said, grabbing her purse and pulling out her cell. She pressed the button, and then scrolled to her phone book. She realized instantly it wasn't her phone. She'd grabbed the wrong cell phone off the pad. "It's Gregory's cell phone."

"Gregory, as in the new downstairs neighbor," Tasha said.

"Gregory, as in the city's management consultant."

"So he finally got here, huh?"

"What, you knew about him?"

"Jac, just about everybody in your office knew about him. Bethany told me. The rumors have been floating around for weeks."

"How didn't I know?" Jacqueline wondered aloud.

"You didn't know because you're always too busy with your work. So you guys work together and live together." She laughed. "Talk about destiny."

"There is no destiny and we don't live together, Tasha. We live in the same building, and it happens all the time. So don't make it a big deal. Nothing happened."

"Nothing happened? Who said anything happened? See, now I know you're hiding something."

"I'm not hiding anything. He just moved here from D.C. His name is Gregory Armstrong. Leland introduced us last night at the reception. He's here to review the city's management and make recommendations, and he was kind enough to let me crash at his place when I locked myself out and couldn't get in touch with you. That's all there is to it. No big deal."

"Uh-huh," Tasha said skeptically, then looked at the cell phone in Jacqueline's hand. She eased it out and started pressing buttons. "So, did you go through his phone book and emails yet?"

"What? No," Jacqueline said, snatching the phone back.

"Why not? Here, give it to me, I'll do it." She reached for it again.

"No." Jacqueline held the phone away. "We're not snooping through the man's phone. I wouldn't want anyone to do that to me."

"It wouldn't matter because your phone book and all your emails are ho-hum boring, just like you. Seriously, girl, you need to shake things up. Start living."

"You know, I do have a life."

"What you have can hardly be considered having a life. I don't know why you deny yourself a little pleasure. When Mom died, you took care of both Dad and me. Now you plan and take care of the whole city. When's it gonna be your turn to find your bliss?"

"I have my bliss. Work is my bliss. I have all I need."

"What about love?" Tasha asked, sadly.

Jacqueline wasn't up for this conversation again. She and Tasha had done it almost weekly. She knew Tasha wanted her to be happy. She just couldn't do it on her terms. "Tasha, it's barely six o'clock in the morning. I'm tired. I don't feel like this right now. It was a long day and an even longer night. I'm gonna crash. Why don't you stay over?"

"I can't, I have a friend in the car. I just stopped by to let you in," she said, heading back to the front door.

"Okay," Jacqueline said, following. "How's school?"

Tasha shrugged. Jacqueline looked at her sternly. She adored her sister, but she hated her lack of focus. She had changed her major three times, and now in a master's program, she was considering yet another change. Just like their father, she never planned past the next minute. "Tasha…" she began in exasperation.

"School is fine, Jac. Chill. Don't get so bent out of shape. Finals are going well. I'm just messing with you." Tasha winked.

Jacqueline just shook her head. "I'll call you later."

"We're still on for next week, right?" Tasha asked, as she headed down the steps, still humored by her joke on her sister.

"Yeah, I'll see you then."

Jacqueline watched her sister get into her car and drive off. She stayed at the window a few minutes longer. Dawn had crept up over the city. Her thoughts wandered. She had too much on her mind. It was the end of the year and work was busier than ever, and with the recent staff reductions she was basically running her office all by herself, with Bethany as her helper now and then.

She turned and headed into her kitchen. She made herself a cup of hot tea and placed it on the small glass table in her sunroom. She sat in one of the cushioned wrought-iron chairs and looked around. The alcove was cozy and comfortable, just right for her work area. She spent many long nights working at this table. It wasn't as extensive as Gregory's office space, but it suited her needs perfectly. As much as she liked Gregory's place, she loved hers.

She opened her laptop and checked her schedule. She revised her list of things to do, adding "Get my phone and return Gregory's phone" to the top. She checked her emails, drafted a few letters to be sent out and then typed a postevent report while everything was fresh in her mind. She yawned again, deciding to lie down a few minutes before starting her day and going to the office. She packed her laptop in her briefcase, grabbed her tea and headed to the bedroom. She changed her clothes and lay down, and a few minutes later she was fast asleep.

It was early, too early. The new city Gregory now called home was still asleep, but he was awake and already out. This was his first morning run in Paradise Cove. He found the running path easily enough. It passed through an open wooden area, circled a man-made lake behind the house and then traversed the perimeter of a newly built golf course nearby. Gregory stretched, then began. Soon he felt his muscles tense and stretch tight as he hit the ground repeatedly. The jarring, pounding sensation of running tuned his senses and helped him refocus. He took quick, deliberate breaths designed to maximize his alertness.

Running had become essential to his well-being. He enjoyed it, and it helped him clarify his thoughts. And after last night, running was mandatory. After a sleepless night, he was tense, edgy and restless. It was as if he'd been given a boost of energy, and it was all because of one person, Jacqueline.

After the kiss, after she had gone into the guest room and closed the door, he had delved full force into the city's entire management structure. He needed the mental distraction. He noted lapses in overall development and financial forecasting and much-needed improvement in strategic planning assessments. But even that didn't get her off his mind.

He nodded to several passing runners as he followed the paved path through the sparse woods. After a while he increased his pace, taking long, deliberate strides. He hoped each step would help to clear his mind. He needed this. He'd been distracted for the first time in five months. His self-imposed abstinence had never troubled him before. He was always in full control. Now, he could feel that control waning fast.

All night, all he could think about was the kiss they shared. It was definitely more than he expected when he challenged her to do something spontaneous. What began as a sweet, chaste kiss ended as an erotic seduction. She started his blood boiling, and it had been on a steady simmer ever since.

When he prepared to go on his predawn run, he was surprised to see her asleep in the living room. She was obviously waiting for someone. He grabbed a throw from his bedroom and covered her before heading out.

Usually when he ran, he didn't use his cell phone's audio feature. He preferred the silence of concentration. He carried his cell for emergencies. Today he decided his downloaded music was just what he needed. It would help him stay focused on his run and not on Jacqueline. Without paying much attention, he hit the play button. To his surprise, his saved music file was completely different. Curious, he stopped running and checked his cell phone. The phone wasn't his.

He continued his run while listening to Jacqueline's downloaded music. It wasn't too bad. When he got back to his condo it was daylight. She was gone, probably back in her own home. He showered, shaved and changed, then went up to Jacqueline's condo. He knocked and waited, but got no answer. He attached a note to her mailbox about her cell phone, then headed out to explore Paradise.

Chapter 8

Jacqueline woke up much later than she expected. There were a thousand things to do and not enough time to do them. Plus, she had experienced another erotic dream. She quickly got herself together and focused on the day ahead. She called her cell phone from her house phone, but got no answer. Then she called the garage. They agreed to come and check out the problem with her car. By the time she showered and dressed for the day, road service came and reattached one of the cable clamps on the car's battery. It hadn't been secured tightly enough, and with the slight jarring from the fender bender it slipped completely loose. Afterward, when she tried calling her cell phone again, there was still no answer.

It was midmorning by the time she got to the office. She walked in hurriedly, sat down and called her cell phone immediately. Gregory still didn't pick up, so she went right to work. After an event as widely publicized and promoted as the mayor's birthday reception last night, she expected her office phone to be ringing constantly. It was. She'd already had ten messages on her office phone, no telling how many she had on her cell phone. She answered calls, made arrangements for interviews and then got started updating projects.

She worked steadily undisturbed for the next hour and a half. Thankfully, her morning got busy and productive with last-minute details from a range of projects she was working on. She was in various stages of putting together three more social events for the mayor and the city, including his annual New Year's Bash. It was already mid-December and that meant holiday parties and events, with the biggest being the year-end celebration.

She continued calling Gregory intermittently throughout the morning. He didn't pick up. By early afternoon it hit her that he probably wouldn't. But if she called her phone number using his cell number, he just might answer. It was worth a try. She grabbed his cell phone from her purse and called. He picked up on the second ring.

"Hello, Jacqueline," he said with charm and ease.

"Gregory?"

"Who else would be answering your cell phone?" His voice was deep and melodious and shot right through her. She instantly remembered the sensation of his moist lips kissing her neck just hours earlier. She shivered at the thought.

"Yes, that's why I'm calling. Obviously I have your phone and you have mine. We need to make an exchange."

"Absolutely. Are you at home now?"

"No, I'm at work," she said.

"At work? It's Saturday afternoon and it's a beautiful day. You should be out enjoying it."

"Some of us still have to work," she said.

"You know what they say, all work and no play—"

"Makes more work for me to do later on," she continued.

He chuckled. The joyous sound of his laughter made her smile. "Okay, I get your point," he conceded. "I can drop by the office and return your phone to you."

She glanced at her watch. If she met up with him now, she'd still have time to get to the hotel and review the contract for the mayor's New Year's celebration. "Perfect. Can you meet me in about ten minutes? I have an appointment in half an hour."

"Probably not," he said, "I'm not in Paradise Cove. I'm about forty-five minutes out."

She glanced at her watch again. "Okay, I have to wrap up a few more things here, and then I'll be at the Paradise Hotel in about an hour. It's where the reception was last night. Can you meet me there?"

"Sure. I'll see you in an hour."

"Okay, thanks," she said, then pressed the end button. She took a deep breath, then shook her head. Gregory Armstrong was pure seduction, and everything about him screamed *caution*. He was every woman's fantasy, and if last night's kiss was any indication, she knew she was headed for trouble. Still, it had been a long time since a man held and kissed her like that.

"Momentary insanity," Jacqueline said aloud, reminding herself again of her affirmation earlier. Maybe, just maybe, she'd convince herself that was what it actually was. But how could it have been momentary insanity when she had known exactly what she was doing? She had initiated it, enjoyed it, and now she wanted it again more than she ever wanted to admit, even to herself.

This was ridiculous. She didn't go in for all the romance-sentimental stuff. She was practical and levelheaded. She didn't let overstimulated sex glands rule her life. Admittedly she was attracted to Gregory. Fine, she'd admit that. But attraction was far from action. All she had to do was forget about the kiss and focus on work. She did. By the time she was ready to leave, she was nicely caught up for Monday morning.

Twenty minutes later, Jacqueline calmly walked into the luxurious Paradise Hotel. She looked around for any sight of Gregory. Fortunately she had arrived first, so she headed to the banquet manager's office to quickly take care of some business. After a brief discussion and a few contract changes, she exited the offices and went back to the lobby. Hopefully Gregory was there by now.

Gregory saw her as soon as he walked into the large lobby. She was standing by the concierge desk. She appeared to be all business with her briefcase and clipboard. She wore a slim navy blue skirt, a white thin-striped shirt and a wide navy belt highlighting her slender waist. She had on high stiletto heels and the same fashionable glasses from the night before. Her hair was pulled back and up into a casual ponytail. She looked like a prim and proper schoolmarm. He liked it on her. Everything about her was pure seduction, even if it wasn't her intention. And it looked as if he'd have to steel himself even more to keep his promise of no interoffice fraternization.

He approached, watching as she jotted something down on the clipboard, then looked up and around. She waved and smiled at several hotel employees as they walked by. Then a man came over to speak to her. Greg paused and waited, sizing the man up instantly: a self-important narcissist. He knew people like that. Jacqueline obviously knew him, and he was definitely attracted to her. He stood too close and smiled too wide. He saw as she casually stepped back, but remained civil and cordial. The man leaned in closer and she stepped back again, then looked around uncomfortably.

Greg took that as his cue to approach. At first he had all intentions of just exchanging phones and going on with his day. The less interaction he had with her after last night at this point, the better. Then he saw that she was obviously uneasy with the man.

He walked over with casual coolness. "Hey, sorry I'm late," Greg said with ease, as he placed his hand possessively on the small of her back and stepped close. She didn't step away.

Jacqueline turned toward him. Her breath caught and her jaw dropped slightly in seeing him. It wasn't just her imagination last night. This man was classically gorgeous. And obviously, there was nothing momentary about this insanity. *Calm down, girl,* she chided herself mentally. "Hi, Gregory," she said breathlessly, not recognizing her own voice for a moment. "You're not late, actually, I'm early."

Greg smiled at her, seemingly captivated. Then, as almost a second thought, he turned and looked at the man still standing with them. "Hi, I'm Greg Armstrong," he said assertively as he extended his hand to shake.

"I'm sorry, Gregory, this is Jason Whitfield. Jason was the city manager for a while."

"Aah, Jason Whitfield, of course." Greg said, recognizing the name instantly. This was the man responsible for getting the city in the major financial chaos it was currently facing, chaos in which he'd been hired to straighten and clean up.

"Armstrong, Armstrong," Jason repeated slowly, as if to ponder the name for any meaningful recollection. "I don't believe I recognize the name. Are you from around here?"

"No," Greg said.

Jason paused, apparently expecting more of an extended response to his question. Greg didn't comply. "It was good to meet you, Jason. Jacqueline, we're over here. Shall we?"

"Sure," she said attentively, then glanced at Jason. "Nice seeing you again, Jason."

Greg nodded and secured Jacqueline's waist even closer, as he guided her toward the lavish dining area across the massive lobby. "Good friend of yours?" he queried, as they walked.

She took a deep breath and nodded. "Yes, from a long time ago. We used to hang out together."

"And now?" he asked.

"And now we don't," she simply said.

"Good, I'm glad to hear that."

Jacqueline smiled inwardly. It was nice being rescued, even if the rescuer didn't realize what he was doing. Seeing Jason again had shaken her up. But seeing his face when Gregory walked up was priceless.

It might be wrong, but she totally enjoyed his being uncomfortable.

"I thought you might be hungry. I have a table waiting and I thought we could talk."

Talking was the last thing she wanted. She knew he wanted to talk about the night before. Jacqueline turned and looked back to the lobby. Jason was no longer there. "Actually, Gregory, I really need to get back to work."

"Okay, but after lunch. You wouldn't want me eating in this beautiful restaurant on my first day here all alone, would you? You're the only person I know here in Paradise Cove, and I hate eating alone."

She smirked. "That's not exactly true. What about your friend the state trooper?"

"Carter lives in Phoenix."

Just then a waiter walked by carrying a crisp Cobb salad and a massive cheeseburger and fries. Her stomach rumbled softly. She took a deep breath, hoping Greg didn't hear it. She was hungry. As usual, she'd forgotten to eat again. She nodded. "Okay, thanks, lunch sounds great. But my treat. I'd like to thank you for last night."

"We'll talk about that part later," Greg said. He turned and nodded to the hostess. She appeared to be watching them and waiting for her prompt. She hurried over and, without a word to Jacqueline, escorted them to a booth away from the lobby area. As they sat, the hostess recited the day's specials, giving particular attention to Greg as she spoke. She smiled and joked, and even leaned in to point out a particular item on his menu. Jacqueline shook her head. Some women are just shamefully obvious. He thanked her, and then ordered California iced teas for both of them before she left.

"What's a California iced tea?" Jacqueline asked.

"Trust me, it's exactly what you need right now."

"Nonalcoholic?" she asked.

"Of course," he said, smiling. "You have to get back to work, right?"

She nodded. He reached into his pocket and pulled out her cell phone. She dug through her purse and got his. They exchanged across the table. "Thank you," she said, sounding relieved.

"No problem. I used to be just like that, attached to my cell. Then I realized there are other things in life to be attached to."

"I'm not attached to my cell," she said defensively.

"My mistake. You're a very popular lady. Your phone hasn't stopped ringing all morning and afternoon. I put it on silent after the first five calls."

"I don't know about popular, but certainly busy. They're all business calls. It's like that after a big event," she said absently, as she began scanning her missed-calls log. There were over thirty-five messages so far.

"Is that such a good idea?"

"What?" she asked, still scanning through the messages.

"Being so busy," he said. "When do you take time to relax?"

"Being busy is a good thing. Besides, it's all part of the job."

"Is it really?" he asked, dipping his head slightly to get her attention. She looked up from her cell phone. The inquisitive tone in his voice got her attention. "You know, I used to think that, too. But I recently found that my job, my old job in D.C., could get along just fine without me being available twenty-four hours a day."

She stopped scanning her phone log and looked up at him more attentively. There was something in his eyes that instantly connected with her. He seemed to know how she felt. A part of her *was* tired of constantly being on call. "I understand what you're saying, but I made a choice a while back. My career comes first."

"At the expense of your personal life and other pursuits?" he asked.

"Yes," she said. Greg shook his head. "You don't agree?"

"It's not that I don't agree. It's that I've been there. Work can't be your only release. It's dangerous. You burn out that way fast."

"I like what I do and I'm good at it."

"I'm sure you do, and I know you're good at it. But logging in extreme hours and sacrificing everything else, including your health, isn't the way to do it."

"That sounds like experience talking."

"I know a thing or two about being a workaholic."

"I'm not a workaholic. I'm just dedicated."

"Working compulsively to the detriment of everything else," he said. "By definition, that's a workaholic."

"No," she said quickly. "That's not me."

"Last night at the reception, everyone was having a great time laughing, joking, talking and enjoying themselves. Not you. You barely looked up from your phone all night."

"That's because I was working."

"Exactly. I bet you're always working."

"So, you were a workaholic, huh? Is that why you left your job in D.C. and came here to Paradise, because you were burned-out?" she asked.

He took a deep breath, assessing her question. This

was not the conversation he expected to have. But he answered anyway. "Not quite, but something like that."

"And do you think coming here might change things for you?"

"I've already changed things for me. I don't work twenty-four seven like I used to."

"Because you're no longer a lawyer?" she surmised.

"No. I'm still a lawyer," he affirmed. His steely eyes never wavered. "But to answer your questions, a friend suggested I come out here, check it out."

"Your friend the state trooper?" she asked.

"No, another friend," he said. "He's a doctor."

"A doctor," she said, interested. He nodded without adding more, so she continued. "And you think I'll lose myself, too, and become a workaholic?"

"What I think doesn't matter. What do you think?"

She considered his question a few seconds. "I think we should order lunch."

"And my other question—when do you take time to relax?" She didn't respond. He nodded knowingly. "That's what I thought."

"I have a question for you," she said, choosing to ignore his statement. "How do you go from attorney to city-management consultant?"

"Being an attorney isn't the only talent I have. I'm a lawyer, yes, but I also mastered in business management."

"So you're a Renaissance man," she quipped.

He smiled. "I don't know about that, but I do have a few noteworthy skills." Just then their waiter arrived with the drinks and to take their food order.

Jacqueline was relieved for the waiter's interruption. She looked back at her menu. She ordered a Cobb salad, and Greg ordered the chef's special grilled chicken and morels in Madeira sauce. When the waiter left they each took a sip of the iced tea. "This is really delicious," she said. "Iced tea and lemonade. I'm going to have to remember this for next time. So, Gregory—" she began.

"Please, my friends call me Greg," he interrupted.

"I think I prefer Gregory."

"Why?" he asked. "Certainly we know each other well enough after last night."

An instant hot flash streaked through her body. Suddenly it was getting warm in the restaurant. "Yes, about last night—" she began.

"No, let's go back to my question. Why not call me Greg? What is it, ex-boyfriend or lover with the same name?"

"No. Greg Armstrong, that's thirteen letters."

"So?" he questioned.

"Thirteen is an unlucky number."

"Ah, such as Friday the thirteenth," he surmised quickly. She nodded. "You know, actually, to most of the world, thirteen is a lucky number," he said. She started laughing. "No, for real, thirteen is a prime number. The first U.S. flag had thirteen stars depicting thirteen colonies. A baker's dozen is thirteen, and Wilt Chamberlin, Shaquille O'Neal and Dan Marino all wore the number thirteen. Also, on a personal note, I sank a hole in one on the thirteenth hole the last time I played golf."

She continued. "And don't forget most high-rise hotels, hospitals and office buildings don't have a thirteenth floor or a room number thirteen. Most cities don't have a thirteenth street or avenue. There's no thirteenth aisle on airplanes or airport gates—"

"Okay, okay, I get it. Gregory would be just fine. My mother calls me Gregory."

"Try not to confuse us," she joked.

"I don't think that's possible," he said.

She grimaced, knowing they had to have this conversation and dreading it. It was inevitable. "Look, Gregory, I just want to get this straight and out in the open. About last night, I think we need to clarify what happened between us."

"I agree, but before you say what you have to say, I just need you to know that I don't usually get involved with the women I work with. So whatever you think is going on between us, isn't. When you kissed me, I was flattered of course, but I think we need to—"

"Wait, excuse me, what?" she said.

"The kiss last night," he explained. "You kissed me. It was obvious that you want me, and I'm flattered, but I can't—"

"Whoa, back up, Romeo. *I* want *you?*"

"Yes, I know," he said, in all seriousness.

She laughed. "You gotta be kidding, right? We kissed each other. It was mutual."

He laughed. "Actually, you initiated the kiss. Why are you being so stubborn about this? It's no big deal. Just admit it. You want me. You're attracted to me."

She looked at him with amusement. "Of all the arrogance."

"That's not arrogance. It's the truth."

"From your point of view," she said.

"From any and every point of view," he shot right back.

"Yeah, you're definitely a lawyer, stubborn and bullheaded. You know exactly how to twist the truth. Okay, cards on the table, I kissed you, I initiated it, yes. Then you pulled me back and you kissed me. That's when we got carried away. I weakened. I admit that. I wanted you and you wanted me. But if you think I'm pining over you now or expect some preferential treatment, you're wrong. Get over yourself. Now, excuse me. I think I'd better go." She bumped the side of the table as she slid around the booth to leave. The salt shaker tipped over. She righted it quickly, pinched some and tossed it over her left shoulder. She took a deep ragged breath and grabbed her purse. "Thanks for returning my phone."

"Jacqueline, wait." He reached over and held her hand before she slipped away. "Don't go," he said. "Please stay. I really want to resolve this. It would be pretty bad to alienate the only person I know in the city," he joked. She half smiled and nodded. "Okay, let's be honest. Cards on the table, as you put it. Yes, you kissed me and I kissed you. There was obviously a lot of heated physical attraction between us."

"*Was?*" she asked. "I mean, if we're being honest?" she sat back down before he could broadcast their moment all over the restaurant.

He nodded. "There *is* obviously a physical attraction between us. Last night we got swept up in a moment of passion. But we're two mature adults. We can handle this."

"What exactly are you saying?"

"We have two choices."

"And they are?" she questioned.

"Either we go with it or we don't."

The words slammed into her like a speeding freight train. They were simple and direct and nearly knocked her down. She took a deep breath, hoping her heart would slow down so she could breathe normally again. "You're talking about a fling, an affair?" He nodded. "Okay, if we decide to *not* go with it?" she asked.

"Then everything stops right here at this table."

"And if we decide the other way?"

"We need to think about that before we go forward."

She considered his suggestions. The same thrill of excitement from the night before returned. This was the ultimate spontaneous experience, and she liked the thrill of it. "How long to think about it?" she asked.

"I have a feeling we'll know."

"Agreed," she said, watching as two very attractive women walked by their table and openly stared at Gregory. He didn't seem to notice, but she did.

"Jacqueline, I'm leaving in a few weeks. If we decide to do this, know that my plans won't change. I have no intention of staying here or coming back."

"Good. That's perfect then."

"Why perfect?" he asked.

"Let's just say that it is, and leave it at that."

"Okay," he said, "so, tell me about growing up in Arizona."

"Wow."

"What?"

"That was a quick topic change. You took me off guard."

He smiled. "I thought it would be better not to dwell on it. It's already the elephant in the room."

She nodded. "Fine, okay, growing up in Arizona. What do you want to know?" she asked.

"Everything," Greg said, as their meals arrived.

Jacqueline smiled. She knew what he was doing, of course. He was trying to put her at ease. The rest of the meal she told him about her beautiful hometown. Greg, in turn, talked about his travels around the world and some fun anecdotes from law school. She was fascinated by all his experiences. Once she let her guard down, their conversations were easy, fun and lively. Surprisingly, she really enjoyed herself. An hour and a half later, they walked back out to the lobby and headed to the exit.

"Are you going back to the office?" he asked.

She glanced at her watch. "Probably, for a little bit. I have a couple of stops to make first."

He looked around. "It's a beautiful day. Are you sure you need to go to work?" She nodded. "Okay. Do you have your valet ticket?" he asked, holding his hand out to her.

"No. I parked on the other side of the hotel."

"Okay, come on, I'll walk you to your car."

"No thanks. I need to stop at the hotel's banquet office and check on a few things before I run errands. So, I guess this is it. Thank you again for lunch. I had a great time."

He handed his valet ticket to the attendant, then turned to her and just stared and smiled.

Jacqueline's stomach started to tingle, and it had nothing to do with the wonderful meal she just had. It was Gregory. He had a way of looking at her that made her insides burn. His eyes were intense, as if he could feel and hear everything going on inside of her. It was as if they'd known each other forever and not just a few hours. But she needed to keep her mind focused. She couldn't get emotional, no matter how he made her feel. He intended to move on and so did she. "You know what? I think you're gonna like living here in Paradise Cove," she said, looking away from his gaze.

"I think I already do."

She turned back. He was still staring, but now his eyes were even more intense. Her heart rate instantly shot up, and every nerve in her body quivered. The temptation was there and they were both fighting it. He yielded first. He leaned in and kissed her tenderly, then he leaned back and shook his head slowly. "This can't happen between us. We can't do this."

"I know, and I agree," she said. "It's best."

"Friends, neighbors, coworkers?" he offered.

She nodded in agreement. "Yes."

"Okay, friend, I'll see you later," he said casually. She nodded. He turned just as the valet pulled up with his Jag. She watched as he pulled off, then she walked back into the hotel and headed for her car. Each step she took she tried to convince herself she didn't want him. But it was a losing battle and she knew it. She did want him and she could see that he wanted her, too. It was only a matter of time.

Greg got in his car and drove off. He shook his head decidedly. He must be crazy to even consider getting involved with a coworker again. His last fiasco should have taught him that. But everything about Jacqueline felt so right and being with her was a true delight. Aside from her Friday-the-thirteenth craziness, she was wonderful. He thought about the suggestion he made.

There was no hesitation on either part. It felt right and whatever decision they made would be right.

Still, he had no idea what came over him. The sudden urge to kiss her came out of nowhere and hit him hard. He didn't plan it. But seeing her standing there in the sunlight ignited his desire. Kissing her did the same thing to his body today as it did last night. It fed a need but not the hunger. He wanted her, and no one else would do. He licked his lips, still tasting the sweetness of her mouth. She had made his body ache all night, and now she was doing it again.

How could one woman arouse him so completely? He knew it wasn't just because of his prolonged abstinence. No, it was her. Everything about her made him want her. He tightened his grip on the steering wheel. He was losing control and he didn't mind. He told her this couldn't happen, but he knew what he wanted. Unfortunately, time wasn't on his side right now.

Chapter 9

Sunday, Monday and Tuesday came and went uneventfully. She didn't see much of Gregory even though, surprisingly, they shared the same office space as she had an extra desk. She wasn't sure if that was by coincidence or by his design, but she was sure that on some level he was avoiding her. When she got to the office the past two mornings she noticed he'd been there late the previous evenings. Oddly enough, she didn't see him around the neighborhood, either.

He was either in Phoenix or with the city council. When he did pop into the mayor's office, it was quick and professional. He had met with each department head and was making major changes. Mostly everyone was okay with his recommendations and proposals. She was pleased about that. She hated to think he'd come to completely disassemble her workplace. It was obvious they were each trying to put the physical attraction behind them. Jacqueline was satisfied everything would work out. Now if she could just stop thinking and fantasizing about him every waking and sleeping moment.

By Wednesday midmorning Gregory and the mayor were still out meeting with the city council. Jacqueline sat at her desk working, then out of the blue, and for no reason she could imagine, her stomach shuddered. Her heart pumped faster and her nerves tingled. A quick image of Gregory kissing her that first night in his bedroom popped into her head. She took a deep breath and released it slowly. That didn't help. The image was still there, this time more complete.

"Hey, Jac, morning," Bethany said, poking her head into the open doorway.

Jacqueline nearly jumped out of her seat as reality slammed into her fantasy.

"Hey, you okay? I didn't mean to startle you. I know how you get when you're focusing on work."

"Work, yeah, that's right, no, I'm fine, good morning," Jacqueline stammered, trying to quickly compose herself.

Bethany swiftly scanned every inch of the office, focusing on the desk next to Jacqueline's. There were several new boxes against the wall and on the credenza. Also, the large, cumbersome desktop computer that normally sat on the desk was now two laptops. "Greg and Uncle Leland just got back. Roger told me they had some kind of breakfast meeting with the city council. Something's up again. I don't know what it is, but it's big. I'm spreading the word that we're meeting in the conference room in fifteen minutes."

Jacqueline nodded. "Okay, I'll see you there." Bethany left to continue her mission, leaving Jacqueline to recuperate. She looked at her watch. It was a few minutes before eleven o'clock.

Her mouth was bone-dry. She grabbed her teacup and sipped. The tea was cold but would have to do. She needed to compose herself. She gathered her notepad and pen, intending to stop by the coffee room and grab a bottle of water before the meeting began. As soon as she picked up her smartphone, it rang. Seeing the caller ID, she answered. "Hi, Tasha, I can't talk right now. I'm headed into a meeting. I'll call you right back."

"Jac, this will only take a few minutes," Tasha promised.

A few minutes to her sister, Tasha, could mean an hour and a half for anyone else. "Tasha, I'm headed out now. Why don't we meet for lunch today?"

"I can't. I'm meeting Dad. He called me yesterday."

"Dad," she said, then signed heavily. "What did he say?"

"That he's a changed man. That he wants to turn his life around. That he loves us and wants another chance."

There was a quick knock on the office door. Jacqueline turned, seeing Bethany and another coworker motioning for her to follow. She nodded and held one finger up. Jacqueline sat on the side of the desk, with her back to the door, and listened to her father's latest drama.

After a less-than-quick recap of their conversation the night before, Tasha ended by saying she felt sorry for him. Jacqueline interrupted, "I can't deal with this right now."

"Jac, I believe him. He sounds different this time. It's

not what he said, but how he said it. He sounds contrite, like he really means it."

"He's said it all before. It's nothing I haven't heard a thousand times. That's what we argued about two years ago. He says he's changed and then we head right back down that same road again. I can't do it."

"I know what you're saying and I understand but maybe this time, maybe—" Tasha began.

"No, no," Jacqueline said emphatically. "I'm not falling for another 'this time' from him. I'm not getting hurt like that again. I put my trust in him and he lets me down. I'm tired of it. I've had enough picking up after him."

"Jac—"

"No, Tasha. You were young. You were the save-the-marriage baby. I remember what it was really like."

"I guess I failed them, then. Just hear him out."

"Tasha, I can't do this. I need to go. I'll call you tonight. We'll talk then."

"He wants to see us," Tasha said soberly.

"No," she said, louder and stronger. "I'll call you tonight." She said goodbye, then ended the call. She was flustered, upset and fighting back tears of frustration. The last thing she needed back in her life was her father. She took a deep breath to gather herself, then stood and turned around. Gregory was standing there watching her.

"Good morning, Jacqueline."

"How long have you been standing there?" she asked.

"Not long." She looked at him in warning. He smiled innocently. "You ready for the meeting?" She nodded, picked up her notepad and headed to the door where he waited. "I grabbed you a bottle of water."

"Thanks," she said, then licked her lips.

"It's been a few days. How've you been?"

"Don't ask."

"Actually, I've been meaning to talk to you. I've been thinking—"

The thought hit her out of the blue. She was angry and upset and needed to release. She needed him. "Okay, how do we do this?" she said.

"Do what?" he asked, then paused. Enlightenment seemed to reach his eyes. "We just let it happen. If it does, fine."

"And if it doesn't?" she asked.

"That's fine, too," he said.

She was just about to respond when the mayor walked up. "Jacqueline, Greg, excellent you're both here," Mayor Newbury said. Both Jacqueline and Greg turned. "The staff meeting is about ready to start. Jacqueline, I know you've been a huge help since Jason left. Now that Greg's here, I'm depending on you to get him up to speed. I expect you two to work very closely together."

"Very closely," Greg said, turning to look at Jacqueline. She glanced at him. "Yes, Mr. Mayor, I'm sure we can manage that."

"We'll be right there, Mr. Mayor," Jacqueline said. Newbury nodded and continued walking. She turned to Greg. "You can't look at me like that," she whispered.

"Like what?" he asked.

"Like we've done something," she whispered.

"We haven't done anything yet." He stepped aside. "Shall we?"

They walked down the hall in silence. Other

coworkers smiled and greeted them as they passed. When they entered the conference room, all heads turned. Greg handed her the bottle of water. Their fingers touched slightly. She tingled. She looked down then guiltily across the room at the others. No one seemed to notice.

The mayor hadn't arrived yet, so everyone was standing around talking. Roger walked over to Greg. They paired off and stepped to the side, talking in hushed tones. Five minutes later the mayor arrived and the meeting began. After the usual discussion the floor was turned over to Greg.

He told everybody that his main focus would be debt and budget reconstruction. Concerns were raised and addressed, and questions were asked and answered. A half hour later everyone filed out of the conference room. The mayor asked Jacqueline and Greg to stay behind.

"Okay, let's get right to it. Jacqueline," Leland began, "there are three upcoming events still on the calendar for this year. As you know, the city council is concerned about the propriety of our recent expenditures. If we keep going as we are, we'll be bankrupt in three months. That leaves another three months to June, the end of the city's fiscal year. With the federal cuts and the state's recent budget cuts and them filtering down to us, we just don't have the finances we need to continue. It's time to trim the fat. You see what I'm saying."

"Mr. Mayor, there's nothing inflated or exaggerated about our spending. Our records are impeccable."

"Yes, I know they are."

"There's nothing on the books this year that wasn't planned for or budgeted on the books last year."

"Yes, I know that, too," Leland said, "unfortunately the books are not what they should be. Jason should have—"

"Mr. Mayor, may I?" Greg offered. Newbury nodded silently. "I'm gonna just cut to the chase. The state's finance department and the city council think we're spending beyond our means with our events planning. With the state's recent cuts and funding caps, we're hard-pressed to continue as is with all three events you have planned for the city to close out the year."

"So you want to trim the budget as much as possible, okay. I'll see what I can do," she said, then opened her folder. "Maybe we can—"

Leland looked to Greg. "No, we need to make deeper cuts. You have three events on schedule until the end of the year."

"You mean cancel one?" she asked, looking up at him.

"Cancel two, keep one, possibly," Greg said quickly, as if the words wouldn't be as difficult to hear. Jacqueline looked at him as if he'd dumped ice-cold water on her head. "The Food and Wine Festival in January and the Hearts Parade in February are already out."

"What, how, no, that's impossible," she protested. "We can't just cancel two already planned and advertised annual events. Money has already been spent. I have contracts with contractors, suppliers and venders."

"We don't have a choice," Greg said.

"Mr. Mayor—"

"I'm sorry, Jacqueline. We all have to bite the bullet on this. I want you and Greg to see what you can do to make this as painless as possible for everyone. It's going to be bad enough when the media gets wind of this. Work out some strategies and best-case scenarios. Let me know the least problematic way to do this."

Greg looked at his notes. "The City's College Scholarship Awards was two weeks ago."

"Yes, it was an awards dinner for the students who deserved it. We award the actual scholarships at the end of the year."

"At this point the scholarships will have to be drastically trimmed."

"Oh no," she said quietly.

"I'm sorry. We don't have a choice," Greg said.

"What about the contracts I've already signed?" she asked.

"That's why Greg is here," the mayor said. "I'm sorry, Jacqueline. I need you and Greg to put your heads together and get me a definitive report by the end of the week. This is top priority."

"Yes, sir," she said despondently.

Greg and Leland shook hands. Leland left, leaving Greg and Jacqueline alone in the conference room. "I need everything you have on the scholarship-awards event—budget, contracts and all to-date expenses."

"Did you know about this before?"

"Yes, most of it."

"And you didn't say anything."

"No."

"Why?"

"We need to get started. I have a meeting with the state comptroller in two hours and I'd like to get a working knowledge of what we're dealing with."

"Everything's in the office," she said, standing and gathering her paperwork. They walked back to their shared office. He went to his desk, removed his suit jacket and sat down. She closed the door and followed him to his desk. "Why didn't you tell me about this the other night?" she asked.

"Would telling you have changed anything?" he asked.

She didn't answer. She couldn't. She didn't know.

"I'm sorry," he said. "There's no other way to balance the city's budget. Every department is taking a hit, but events planning is the most superfluous."

"Superfluous?" she repeated indignantly.

"Sorry, wrong choice of words," he said. "It's the least essential to the city's future finances."

"That's not much better. Do you have any idea what I do?"

"Yes, I do," he said. "And you do it extremely well. But I still have to cut the events for the good of the whole city."

She nodded. She hated that she understood, and it didn't make her feel any better.

"Jacqueline, it's not personal. It's what I have to do to help the city, your city."

"I understand. It's business."

He nodded and smiled. "I'm glad you understand. Now let's see exactly what we have and what we can save."

She walked over to her desk and gathered and grabbed several files. She handed them to him, identifying and explaining each one in as much detail as possible. Then she went back to her desk and sent him the accompanying computer files and information. In less than two hours' time Greg had a complete and comprehensive working knowledge of each event and their importance to the city's future planning and growth commitments. Each was an annual event, and each year the attendance rate had grown considerably, far exceeding the projected numbers.

Jacqueline was right. Each one of these events would increase the city's exposure and tourism, plus add much-needed revenue to the bottom line. But the problem still remained—something had to be cut.

"You've done an incredible job with these. I can see why the mayor thinks so highly of you."

"Thanks, but I guess that doesn't matter now, does it?"

"You really love this city," he said.

She nodded. "Yes, I do. It's my home."

"Did you ever think about living someplace else?"

"No, why would I? What's better than living in Paradise?"

"That sounds like the city's next promotional idea."

"I don't think we could afford it," she said sarcastically, standing and going back to her desk.

"Probably not," he said, putting his jacket on and gathering what he needed for his next meeting. "I wish there was something else I could do." He walked over to the door to head out.

"There is something you can do," she said, looking at the files on his desk. "Give me my scholarship money back. You're new. You don't have a clue about what's important to the people of Paradise Cove. To you this is all just one big chopping block. You see the bottom line and that's all you care about but these scholarships are important to the kids here. They need them."

"There's nothing I can do." Greg opened the door and left for his meeting.

She felt as if her heart had been ripped apart. She'd

been targeted and there was nothing she could do. Or maybe there was. She dived into her work and skipped lunch while reviewing all her paperwork again. The scholarship program was her immediate concern. Having been a past recipient of the mayor's scholarship, she knew how important each and every dollar was to the students. She spent the rest of the day trying to come up with ideas. Unfortunately, none of them were particularly encouraging.

It was late when she decided to leave for the day. Most of the City Hall employees had already gone home. She packed her briefcase and closed the office door, hoping tomorrow would be better.

Chapter 10

After running a few errands, she headed home. As soon as she drove up she noticed Greg's car was already there. She pulled into her space just as her cell phone rang. Seeing the caller ID, she turned off the ignition and answered. "Hello."

"Hi, neighbor, I need a favor," Greg said.

She looked up through the front windshield. Gregory was standing in his doorway watching her. "A cup of sugar?"

"No."

"What's the favor?" she asked.

"I made too much food, now I'm stuck. Are you hungry?"

"Toss it, freeze it," she suggested easily.

"That would be wasteful, not a good idea," he said simply. "It's dinner, that's it."

"Dinner, huh?" she said, getting out of the car carrying her briefcase and purse. She was hungry, having skipped lunch, and had intended to toss something in the microwave. "What kind of food did you order, Chinese, Japanese, Italian, Thai or pizza?"

"None of the above. I cooked," he said proudly.

She laughed. "You cooked."

"Do you doubt my culinary abilities?"

"Oh heavens, no, I remember, you're a Renaissance man," she said, still chuckling. "I'm sure you're an excellent cook. So what are we having, Cheerios or Frosted Flakes?"

It was his turn to laugh. "Neither, I cooked grilled salmon, asparagus and lemon-herb couscous."

"Umm, sounds good. But truthfully, I was gonna grab something quick and get some work done," she said, using her hip to close the car door. She walked up the path to their shared house.

"Are you sure?" he asked.

She reached the open vestibule. He leaned casually against his door frame as he watched her approach. She took the phone from her ear and disconnected. He did the same. She looked at him and shook her head. "What am I going to do with you?"

He smiled knowingly. "I have a few ideas."

She shook her head. "Gregory, are you flirting with me?"

"Yes, I am."

She walked toward the steps leading to her upstairs condo. She took two steps up, and turned and leaned on the rail. "Why are you so tempting?" she said, then wished she could take it back.

"Tempting." He smiled wide and nodded. "I like that.

It's nice to know. Come." He turned and walked back into his condo, leaving the door open for her to follow.

Jacqueline stood on the step a moment. She closed her eyes and shook her head. She knew exactly what was going to happen. They were going to eat a wonderful dinner and then they were going to make love. Her heart raced and her body tingled in anticipation. He did this to her without a single touch. The door was open. All she had to do is walk through it. She took a deep breath, turned off her rational mind and walked inside.

Gregory was in the dining room lighting candles. The table was set for two with sparkling glassware and monogrammed china. He looked up and smiled, obviously having fully expected her to follow him inside. She walked over and ringed her finger around the rim of a glass. "Wow, the table's beautiful. I guess I was a foregone conclusion, huh?"

"Not at all, but I'd hoped. I'm glad you're here."

"Me, too," she said. "Do you mind if we not talk about work tonight?"

"Sounds like a good idea." He walked over, took the purse and briefcase from her hands and placed them on a side chair against the wall. He took her hand and guided her to sit. After pouring them each a glass of white wine, he served and they ate. The meal was perfection. The conversation was stimulating. The wine was delicious and Gregory was intoxicating. After dinner, they sat and talked more. After a while the conversation slipped into an easy silence.

"There's something, isn't there, Jacqueline? You feel it too, don't you?" he said quietly.

She looked across the table into his warm brown eyes. He was already gazing at her. Their eyes connected and held just like the first time they saw each other. He was right; there was something there, for both of them. It was nothing that was said or done, but it was there. They both knew it. She nodded. "Yes."

"I know this'll sound like a pickup line, but when I look at you I start to feel…" He stopped and took a deep breath, then exhaled slowly.

"Yeah, me, too," she said breathlessly. And that was her problem. She was starting to feel too much. He made her feel the need for other possibilities in life. That was a distraction. Her focus on her goal wavered when Gregory was around, like now. "I think we need to change the subject. You know, you never did answer my question back at the restaurant."

"What question was that?"

"You were a lawyer. How did you go from lawyer to management consultant? Were you disbarred?"

"No."

"Then what?" she asked.

He debated a moment whether or not to tell her. But in an instant, the choice was simple. "A year ago I took stock of my life and decided I needed to make some changes. I took a year off from the law and began exploring my options. Management consultant was one of those options." He reached over, picked up the bottle of wine and refilled her glass. After he put it down he pulled her chair out. "Why don't we go into the living room?"

"Okay." She got up, walked over to the sofa and sat down. He followed, handing her the glass, then sat in the chair across from her with a large coffee table between them. Soft jazz music played throughout the house. The fireplace was lit and candles burned on the mantle. The ambiance was the perfect seduction. She took a sip of her wine. "Dinner was delicious. You're an excellent cook," she said.

"Thanks. I'm still learning. Do you cook?"

"Sometimes, not as much as I'd like to," she said, taking another sip of her drink.

He nodded. "Will you cook for me sometime?"

She smiled shyly and half nodded. "Maybe, we'll see."

There was a comfortable silence as she looked around the room then into the fire. She hadn't really noticed it earlier. There was no wood or gas logs. The flickering, dancing flames seemed to burn from sparkling glass. It looked as if the glass itself was on fire and melting right before her eyes, but it didn't. She sat her glass down, then stood and walked over to the fireplace. "This is stunning. I've never seen a glass fireplace before. It looks like sparkling diamonds. How is it done?"

"It's a specially formulated tempered glass. No odor, no smoke, very safe and efficient. Tell me about Jason," he asked, changing the subject.

She turned and looked back at him. "What about him?" she asked curiously.

"Did he break your heart or did you break his?" he asked.

"It was mutual. Jason was a while ago. He made a choice and so did I. What about you—any relationship heartbreaks lately?"

"None so anyone would notice," he said guardedly.

"So I guess that would make you a heartbreaker, huh?" She saw his jaw tense as he looked away. She noted that perhaps she'd hit on something.

"No, that would make me cautious," he said openly.

"And me reckless for being here with you tonight." She stepped away from the fireplace and started looking around the room. She casually walked to the front window and looked out.

He watched every movement. "It's dinner. It doesn't have to be anything more."

She turned to him. "We both know better than that. Don't we?" She slowly walked around the back of his chair then continued back to the sofa.

"Do you still want him?" he asked.

She picked up her glass and sat back down. It took a moment to realize he was asking about Jason again. "No, definitely not."

"Good answer. But he still wants you," Greg said, smiling.

"I think you're wrong about that one," she assured him.

"I watched him with you the other day. It was obvious."

"You watched us." He nodded. "Why?"

"Call it male curiosity. He wants you."

She smiled and chuckled softly. "What makes you so sure about that?"

"Testosterone intuition. It was in his eyes, his body language, his voice."

"I didn't see or hear anything like that."

"You wouldn't, but it was there and very implicitly stated. Two men and one attractive woman standing in a hotel lobby. Believe me, I know."

"You got all that in just a few minutes," she said.

"Sounds like you two were marking your territory or something. Very primal."

"Yes, very primal," he said fiercely, never breaking eye contact as his eyes narrowed in intensity.

She felt as if her insides were struck by lightning. She could feel her heart palpitate in her chest. A sudden surge of heat shot through her body. Every nerve ending in her body tingled. She felt like the glass fire, burning but still whole. Taking a deep breath, she nodded her head slowly. She understood. "Is that why you kissed me when we were out in front of the hotel? Were you marking me as your territory?"

"That's not my style. And you know exactly why I kissed you, don't you?"

He was right. She knew the answer. She just couldn't say it out loud. He nodded slowly, knowing she knew. His gaze focused with certainty.

She swallowed hard. This flirtation was getting way too intense. She couldn't handle it. "Gregory, this isn't me. I don't just jump into bed with a man I don't know. I'm not that kind of woman."

"I realize that. If you were, we would have been in bed all last weekend."

She shivered, believing him. "That's pretty arrogant."

"Not really."

"So, is that what makes this flirtation thing between us so provocative and enticing to you? I'm a challenge or a conquest yet to be conquered, or is it that you want to get your feet wet in a new city and I'm convenient?"

"You're neither and you know it. If I wanted to 'get my feet wet,' as you call it, I'd have no problems doing it. And that is not arrogance. That's a fact."

"Yeah, that I believe," she said, remembering the women staring at him in the lobby and at the lunch table, and the hostess's obvious overtures.

"You know what? I think you need more fun in your life."

"Do you?" she asked. "Well, since you don't really know me, how—"

"—how can I suggest to you?" he asked.

"Yes, something like that," she said.

"I know the signs. You walk a tightrope of perfection every day. Your biggest fear is that one day you'll fall and everything around you will tumble, as well. You're burning out. You need excitement, freedom. You're trapped and scared. That's why this is so intriguing."

He looked deeply into her eyes. "Let yourself go, Jacqueline. Don't be scared."

"I can't," she confessed solemnly. She was afraid.

"Yes, you can. Wanting doesn't make you weak."

"I'm not that aggressive," she stammered, looking for a way out.

"Yes, you are. You just don't know it yet. For instance, tell me what you want right now."

"You," she said softly. Her heart started beating like a snare drum. She could do this. She stood up and slowly pulled her shirt hem free from her skirt, then began unbuttoning it.

His sensuous lips tipped. He watched intently as her slender fingers slowly slipped each button from the hole. When she finished she walked over to stand in front of him. She reached her hand down to him. He stood and lightly touched the back of his knuckles to her neck, then her chest and finally her breasts. He gently stroked the soft mounds, letting his fingers circle her hardening nipples. He wrapped his arm around her and gathered her close in one smooth motion. They began to move to the soft music.

"You are so beautiful," he whispered, as he grasped her ponytail clip. He unsnapped it, setting her hair free. It tumbled to her shoulders in waves and half curls. He smiled with delight and buried his face to her neck. "You have no idea how long I've wanted to do that. Set you free."

"Tell me this isn't a mistake," she said.

"I can't and I won't lie to you. I just know that I can't get you out of my mind. The first moment I saw you, I couldn't take my eyes off you. I've never been consumed like this before."

"Me either. My sister would say we're flirting with destiny," she said.

"Do you want me, Jacqueline?" he asked in all sincerity.

She nodded.

"No, I need you to say it."

"Yes, Gregory, I want you. I don't know where this is coming from, I can't help myself. It's like I'm drawn to you. I'm falling and I can't stop. I don't want to stop."

He nodded. "I know the feeling," he said, kissing her neck.

The deep reverberation of his voice and the hot warmth of his breath made her shudder inside. His body moved against hers. She could feel every nuance of his arousal. The slow, seductive dance continued. She closed her eyes and laid her head on his chest. He held her tight. His embrace was intense and all-consuming. She felt as if she could stay in his strong arms forever. She knew this was just a fantasy, but for tonight she'd take it. "Just one night," she whispered. "No ties, no strings, no commitments."

"Whatever you want, Jacqueline," he said. Her name tumbled from his lips with ease.

There was no need for formality. They both knew exactly what they wanted. He cupped the back of her head and kissed her. Her world instantly exploded. His tongue went deep, dancing and stroking the inside of her mouth. Then he nibbled her ear, her chin, her neck. She reeled with every sensation imaginable. She never knew a kiss could do all this to her body. Then his mouth returned to hers. She moaned her pleasure as soon as he entered again. Slowly, with languishing ease, the kiss ended. He held her face and looked deep into her eyes.

"Are you sure you're ready for me?" She nodded quickly.

"Come with me." He took her hand; she followed. He led her through the dining room and kitchen, down the hall to his bedroom. Once there, he kissed her tenderly while removing her open shirt. He turned her around to unzip her skirt. He eased it down and smiled, seeing the beauty of her body for the first time. She stood in bra, panties and stilettos. She was breathtaking, much more than he dreamed. "You are so beautiful."

"I believe you already said that," she said shyly.

"It bears repeating."

She reached up to unbutton his shirt. When she finished she opened it wide. His chest was magnificent. She touched him, remembering the first time she saw him like this. "Nice."

He took her hand and kissed it lovingly. "Lie down

on the bed," he instructed. She sat on the side of his bed and then lay back.

"I'll be right back."

Jacqueline smiled happily as she took a deep breath and looked up at the ceiling. This was really happening. She was going to do this. It was out of character, it was unlike her, but she needed and wanted it. Jason had been the last, and that was a long, long time ago. She closed her eyes, relaxing into the comfort of his bed. Just like in the guest room, it was totally comfortable.

"Jacqueline."

She opened her eyes to see that he hadn't undressed, but the room had darkened. She sat up on her elbows to look at him.

"Lie on your stomach."

She didn't move.

"Trust me," he assured her. "I would never hurt you."

She looked at him and nodded, then rolled over. He sat down beside her, touching her shoulders and her back, and feeling the roundness of her rear before stroking the length of her bare legs. Her heart beat wildly as his hands traced all along her body. It felt so good to be touched and caressed like this. Then he began rubbing her with a more deliberate intensity. She felt a warm liquid drip to her skin. He rubbed it across her back and began massaging it into her shoulders. His hands were firm and gentle. She moaned at the pleasure of his touch. Her muscles and body gave way and completely relaxed.

"May I?" he asked. Before she could register what he asked, he'd already unsnapped her bra. She leaned up and he pulled it free. She stretched and folded her arms to rest her head on her hands. He continued. Every nerve ending in her body tingled and relaxed.

The full-body massage was exactly what she needed. Every inch of her body craved attention, and he delivered over and over and over again. She didn't know when it happened, but it did. The soft music, the subdued lighting, the warmth of the heated oil and the gentle massage together relaxed her to sleep. The last thing she remembered was Gregory leaning over and kissing her back, then her shoulder. "To be continued," he whispered, as she drifted off to sleep.

Chapter 11

They didn't do it.

Greg lay in bed alone, looking up at the ceiling. He knew her bedroom was right above his. He'd seen the building's blueprints when he chose it. He wondered if she was having as hard a time sleeping as he was. Waking up alone was usual for him. He never stayed over and seldom allowed anyone else to. But he didn't expect to be alone this morning. He didn't know when she'd gotten up and left, but she did. It was the second time she left his apartment in the middle of the night. He smiled, considering the idea of getting a security lock on his bedroom door.

He shook his head, not believing what he was doing. He was knowingly getting involved with another coworker. Granted, this situation was completely different and it wasn't permanent. He'd be leaving in a few weeks, but still, it went against what he promised himself. But maybe Carter was right. Maybe it was time to let go of the past. What happened was because of one woman. Jacqueline was certainly nothing like her.

He smiled in the darkness. He had always been extremely selective when it came to the women in his life. When they gave willingly, he took graciously. But Jacqueline was different. He liked the idea of waiting for her. She had said she was ready for him, but he knew she wasn't. And if they'd been together she would have regretted it, hated herself and him, too. He couldn't do that. He rolled over and closed his eyes, but sleep wasn't coming. A short while later he got up, went into the bathroom and grabbed a cool shower.

He set the shower head to deep massage. The jets beat onto his body with savage rage. He needed this. Ten minutes later he grabbed a towel and dried off. He exited the bathroom and walked over to the dresser. As soon as he reached for clothes his cell rang. He grabbed it quickly, thinking it might be Jacqueline, then seeing the caller ID, it was. "Hello," he said, sitting down on the bed naked.

"Hi, um, how are you?" she said haltingly.

Greg smiled. He lay back on the pillows and folded one arm beneath his head. He looked up at the ceiling again. "Good morning," he said more lazily.

"I wasn't sure if you were awake yet."

"I'm awake. I couldn't sleep," he said.

Jacqueline paused a moment to gather herself. She had no idea what prompted her to call him. She had debated about doing it for the past hour and a half, ever since she got back to her apartment. "Apparently I could. I fell asleep on you," she confessed needlessly.

"Yes, I know, that was the whole idea," he said. "You needed the relaxation."

"I don't think I've ever felt more relaxed in my life. Your hands are lethal."

He laughed. "In that case, I'm happy to have been of service. Let me know when you want another one."

"I might take you up on that."

"Anytime, anyplace, any position."

Jacqueline flushed. This was getting to be a habit. "Where are you?" she asked.

"I'm in bed. You?" he answered and asked.

"I'm in bed, too," she nearly whispered. "I woke up with your shirt on. Have any idea how that happened?"

"Yes, I put it on you."

"I'll make sure to get it back to you."

"No rush. Is that what you're wearing now?"

"No, I just got out of the shower."

"Me, too." He looked up again. His mind rushed to the visual instantly. His body, already aroused from before, began to harden again. "Perhaps we should have conserved water and showered together."

"Gregory—" she began.

"Listen," he interrupted, "I'm headed out for a run, why don't you join me?"

"No, I can't, maybe another time."

"Okay, I'll see you later."

"Gregory, um, one more thing," she said.

"Yes."

"About last night, did we..." she began, then paused.

"Have sex, make love?" he offered.

"Yes."

"No, we didn't," he said, and then heard her open sigh of relief. "You sound relieved."

"I am. I would hate to have no memory of us being together. I'll talk to you later. Have a good run. Bye."

Gregory chuckled to himself as he pressed the end button on his cell. This flirting thing was nice. He liked the seductive conversations they had. Sitting up, he quickly dressed and grabbed his cell. He stepped outside to the beginning of a bright beautiful day. The weather was amazing. It was mid-December and the temperature was heated up past seventy. This was certainly nothing like living in D.C. or New York. He took a deep breath, stretched and began his run. Thoughts of Jacqueline followed him all the way.

They didn't do it.

Jacqueline was still stunned. She woke up in Gregory's bed, curled up close against his body. He was completely dressed except for his shirt, and his arm was draped protectively around her waist. She had on his shirt and her panties. Slipping out of his bed was the only thing she could think to do. She'd obviously fallen asleep—how embarrassing was that?

She headed to work early and worked feverishly trying to get alternatives to supplement the scholarship money. She failed miserably. Unfortunately, most scholarship gifts had already been delegated. She also worked on cutting the budget of the final three events in hopes of saving them all. She was failing there, too. By early evening, after another long day, she decided to head out and take the night off. She fixed herself a quick salad for dinner. Afterward, she relaxed in the living room with a book she'd been trying to read for the past month and a half.

After reading the first few pages she heard footsteps. She looked up and turned as soon as she heard the knock on her door. She knew it was Gregory. She opened it and saw him standing there and smiling. "Hi," she said, more enticingly than she expected.

"Would you believe I locked myself out?" he joked.

She smiled. "No, I wouldn't."

"I didn't think so. Actually I thought I'd go for a walk and since you're the only person I know in the neighborhood, I thought maybe you'd join me."

"I can't. Sorry."

"More work?" he questioned.

"Actually—" she began.

"Don't worry about it. I'll see you later."

"Okay, see ya," she said, then slowly closed the door. She closed her eyes and leaned her forehead on the door frame. Resisting him was getting harder and harder. She listened as his footsteps receded farther and farther away. Maybe she should just... A split second later she grabbed her keys and opened the door. By the time she hurried down the steps, she saw Gregory in his car backing out of the driveway. He stopped as soon as he saw her.

Jacqueline hesitated before hurrying over. He rolled the window down. "Change your mind?"

"Yeah, I thought you were going for a walk."

"I am. Come on, hop in."

She did. The walk turned into an impromptu drive and tour of Paradise Cove. It was a small city, but it had been growing steadily the past few years. Jacqueline told

Greg its history, how it was originally settled shortly after the Civil War. They skimmed the outskirts and eventually drove to the small lake on the other side of town. He parked. They got out and started walking.

"I've been wondering. How did you get to be so superstitious about Friday the thirteenth?"

"I wouldn't call it superstitious," she said. "I'm just cautious."

He looked at her already knowing better. She looked at him, questioning. "What?"

He smiled. "Okay, you're cautious. Why is that?"

"Things have a tendency to happen to me on that day."

"Such as what?"

"Such as everything that's ever gone wrong in my life has happened on that day," she said.

"That sounds pretty ominous. What happened last Friday?"

"As usual the day started off crazy. Well, maybe not crazy, but definitely unlucky. My alarm didn't go off, so I woke up late. Then my newspaper arrived soaked, even though there wasn't a cloud in the sky."

"Both easily explained," he interjected.

"Oh, then my almost brand-new laptop computer, in excellent working condition Thursday night, suddenly died, and my home phone service went out completely. Then my car battery died after I got it out of the shop the day before. Finally, the reception I put together went sideways—"

"Sideways how?" he asked, having firsthand knowledge that the mayor's reception was a great success.

"The band got stuck in traffic, the flowers arrived wilted and dying and we had to change them out at the last second. The menu changed at the last minute, and two bartenders called in sick. And to top my day off, I nearly hit a black cat darting in front of me, my new neighbor parks in the wrong space and I run into the back of his car, a black Jaguar. Now, all that might not seem like much to you, but to me, it was definitely a Friday-the-thirteenth thing."

Greg had begun chuckling as Jacqueline described her crazy day. "I'm sorry. I'm not laughing at you. I'm just laughing at everything that happened. But still, you have to admit all that craziness can and could happen any day of the month, right?"

"Yeah, but it didn't. They all happened last week, Friday the thirteenth."

"With all that, I'm almost afraid to even ask about the last Friday the thirteenth."

"I broke up with Jason. He sent me an email."

"Ouch."

"Actually, in hindsight, it was a good day," she said with a laugh.

"Okay, you're not gonna give up on your superstitions. So I'm not even going to try and talk you out of them."

"Smart move," she said, nodding justifiably, having stated her case and made her point.

"You know, there was one good thing that happened on Friday the thirteenth," he said.

"What's that?"

"It's the day we met."

She eyed him suspiciously. "Yeah, I'm not sure if that's a good thing or a bad thing yet. That jury's still out."

He laughed out loud as he pulled her into his embrace.

They walked in silence a few minutes as he wondered just how superstitious she really was.

"Let's go over here," he said, guiding her toward the empty playground area. Jacqueline headed right to the swings and sat down. Greg sat on the swing next to her in the opposite direction. She pushed off and began swinging and laughing. She soared higher and higher, laughing and giggling the whole time. Greg watched in admiration. It was different seeing her like this. She was carefree, happy and joyful. After a while she slowed the swing to stop. She was breathless while still smiling. "You look so beautiful doing that, like you don't have a care in the world. Definitely not the woman I met Friday night."

"The woman you met Friday night was working," she said.

He turned, twisting and crossing his swing chains to face her. "The woman I met Friday night needs to have more fun."

"I have responsibilities," she said, leaning her head to the side, and then looked away. "I've always had responsibilities," she added, trying not to sound despondent.

"That sounds burdensome."

She brightened and sat up again, yet the smile on her face never reached her eyes. "Nothing I can't handle."

"You, Ms. Murphy, definitely need to swing more." He reached out and pulled her swing toward his. Holding the linked chains together, he leaned over and kissed her tenderly. Afterward he took a moment to just look into her eyes. Soft and brown, they told a silent story of pain and heartache, but also of perseverance and hopefulness. He knew right then Jacqueline was someone special.

She stood and walked to the sliding board. "So, you run, huh?" she asked.

"Yeah, I just started again. I used to do it years ago."

"Why'd you stop?" she asked, turning to see that he was still sitting on the swing.

"I got busy. Work started taking more and more of my time, and I got distracted by other things." He stood and walked over to her.

"Do you like being a lawyer?" she asked. They continued walking together and left the play area.

"Yes. I do. I actually believe in truth and justice."

"That's very Justice League of you. But you forgot, the 'and the American way' part."

He laughed. "Oh wow, a beautiful woman who knows her comic books. I like that."

"They're called graphic novels," she corrected, falling in step beside him.

"That's right," he said, while still chuckling. "So, I guess you have brothers, then."

"No, actually I read them as a child. I always wanted superpowers. I wanted to be Justice Girl," she said proudly.

"Justice Girl," he chuckled. He stopped walking and sat down on the side bench overlooking the lake. She sat beside him. "I like that. What would her powers be?"

"I never really got that far into the whole fantasy equipment or superpowers part. I was about ten at the time. I knew she would have superstrong powers, and nobody would ever be able to hurt her or her sister." She paused, feeling deep emotions saturate her heart, then took a deep breath to reaffirm her strength. "She would always make everything right. Life would be perfect.

Kids would be happy, and mothers and fathers would never leave them." The fantasy flowed from her lips.

He paused. "I'm sorry. Your parents passed away?"

"Actually," she said softly, "my mom and dad divorced. We lived with my mom for a little while. Then she was in a car accident and died instantly, killed by a drunk driver."

"I'm so sorry," he whispered, draping his arm around her shoulders.

"Thank you." Her voice trembled noticeably. "I felt as if I had died also. I was so lost. I had no control, no plan, nothing. After that my sister and I went back to live with my dad."

"I know exactly how you felt. My father died when I was young. He had a heart attack at work and nobody noticed because he was still at his desk."

She looked up at him. "I'm sorry."

He nodded. "How old were you?" he asked softly.

"I was sixteen, my sister was eleven."

"So your dad raised you."

"Hardly. My dad's an addictive gambler. That's why my mother left him. The problem is he loses all the time. He was a lawyer, too. He lost his business, the cars, everything. The only reason we still had the house was because it wasn't in his name. But it didn't matter—he was mostly gone anyway."

"Where was he, Las Vegas?"

"Actually he was in prison for almost five years for filing false tax returns and tax evasion."

"I'm sorry. But wait, how did you survive if he was away?"

"We did okay, I managed to finish school early and

I got a job. I worked during the day and had college classes at night."

"That must have been really hard."

She nodded. "It was. I was scared most of the time 'cause I never knew what to expect. We couldn't plan anything. But I got used to it. I had no choice. I had to be the responsible one and take care of everything. By the time social services found out that my dad wasn't there and my sister and I were living on our own, I had just turned eighteen and could legally take care of her. I've been doing it ever since."

"That was a lot of responsibility for someone so young. You should be very proud of yourself."

She shook her head. "I can't believe I'm telling you all this. I never told anyone about Justice Girl."

"I'm glad you told me," he whispered, leaning in. "And don't worry, your secret is safe with me." He wrapped his arms around her and held tight. After a while they stood and started walking again.

"Did any of that happen on Friday the thirteenth?"

"Still trying to figure that out, huh?" she asked. "Yes, as a matter of fact, they all did. The divorce was finalized on the thirteenth and my mom died on the thirteenth."

"I'm beginning to see your point."

She nodded. "So, changing the subject, you said you were distracted by other things. I assume you mean a woman."

"Yes," he said. She wanted to know more, but she decided not to ask. "The question you're trying to figure out how to ask me tactfully is whether or not we're still together. The answer is no."

"I gather it wasn't a good ending," she said.

"Actually it *was* a good ending. It was mutual, more or less."

"Meaning she wanted marriage and you didn't."

He started laughing. "How'd you come to that conclusion?"

"That's what happened, isn't it?"

He looked at her, amazed. She was pretty much on target. "Yes, she wanted marriage, but more for what I could offer her than for me."

"Oooh, a gold digger," she said.

"No, not a gold digger—she's got plenty of money in her own right. Basically she's smart and knows an opportunity when it presents itself."

"So you're an opportunity. Hmm, I guess I'd better keep that in mind. Just in case," she joked. "So tell me, Mr. Opportunity, what are you, superrich and powerful or something?"

He chuckled. "Yeah, or something."

"I figured that. The Jag, the condo—you had to have at least some money to afford all that, plus your decorator."

"And what about you? Is money majorly important to you?"

"No, not really, I live comfortably enough. More money means more drama. My younger sister married a very wealthy guy a few years ago. She was twenty at the time. It lasted about a month. His family was livid when they found out. They wanted an annulment. She refused, her husband buckled, so she accepted a divorce."

"She got alimony," he surmised.

"No, it was never about the money. But his parents

couldn't see that. My sister actually fell in love, so did he. But money got in the way."

"Not exactly the perfect fairy-tale ending of a happily-ever-after romance."

"No, but then reality never is." They got back into his car and drove home. They walked to the open vestibule and paused. "Coffee?" he offered.

"No thanks." She smiled happily. "That was a lot of fun. I haven't been on a swing in years."

"I guess I have to make sure I get you a swing in the yard."

"Sounds good. I had a really good time tonight. Thanks for the walk. I think I needed that, to get out for a while."

"You're welcome," he said. He reached out and took her hand. She knew exactly what was going through his mind. It was the same thing she was thinking about. "Jacqueline…"

Her inner struggle was evident. A part of her wanted to let go and be free with him. Another part of her wanted to hold control for fear of losing everything. She glanced up the steps, seeing her escape. Control won out. "I gotta go. It's late, way past my bedtime."

"Want some company?"

"Stop tempting me," she said, smiling.

"Good night, Jacqueline."

"Good night, Gregory."

"Let me know if you change your mind," he joked, then stepped in and kissed her lips tenderly. When their lips parted, they stood a moment just looking into each other's eyes. "Are you sure you don't want to come in for a coffee?" he asked.

She shook her head, knowing that if she stayed any

longer she'd give in to her desire. "Good night," she said, and walked up the stairs slowly. Each step seemed harder and harder to take as the battle raging inside her continued. She wanted to be with him, but the fear of letting go was too strong. She opened her front door and turned around. Greg was still standing at the lower landing watching her.

Their eyes held in earnest. Everything she ever wanted was there. All she had to do was call to him. Then the feeling swept over her. She knew she was going to surrender to the flood of passion between them. She was falling for him. It happened so fast, almost the instant she saw him. It was crazy, it was reckless, but it was true. All she could think about since meeting him was: what would it be like to be with him?

Now, just once, she wanted to let go. She licked her lips, still tasting the sweetness of him. Her heart sputtered as she held her breath, then exhaled his name. "Gregory," she called out softly, and smiled. He turned and looked up. "I changed my mind."

Chapter 12

Greg walked up the steps toward her.

Jacqueline backed up into her apartment as he stepped through the threshold and closed the door. "I need you to make love to me, Gregory," she whispered. "Slow, and all night long."

He caressed her face in his hands and kissed her tenderly. "Slow, and all night long," he promised.

She smiled, turned and walked through the living room to the dining room. Greg followed her as she entered the kitchen. With the lights dimmed, he watched as she pulled out a bottle of wine and two glasses. She took them to the side counter, then poured.

He watched. Her back was to him. His mouth watered, seeing the taunt, apple roundness of her rear in her jeans. Her ample bottom called to him. All he wanted to do was touch her, feel her and taste her. He walked over and pressed himself close, bracing his hands on the cool marble on either side of her body. He picked up a glass and tipped it to her lips. She sipped. Afterward he brought the same glass to his mouth and sipped. Then he put it down and shifted her hair to the side. He dipped his mouth to her neck and kissed her. "I dreamt about you last night," he whispered near her ear.

"Did you," she said. Feeling him this close was electrifying. Her body began to simmer. She'd never felt like this before. She'd wanted him since the first moment she saw him. Now he was here with her. It was her time.

"Mmm-hmm," he hummed, as he kissed her neck again and pressed his body even closer. Her stomach fluttered and did somersaults. She could feel his warm breath on her neck and shoulder. She could also feel his arousal pressed close to her back as he continued kissing her.

"What did you dream?" she rasped huskily. Her voice was barely recognizable.

"We were in a kitchen like this. And I kissed you like this." He tipped her head to the side and kissed her passionately. Then he continued kissing her ear, her lobe, her neck and shoulders. She felt her body move, grinding back against his. He pressed closer as each kiss intensified. Her body burned with desire from the inside out. She reached back to hold him. Her hand hit one of the glasses and spilled wine. She reached for a towel, but he took her hand instead. Leaning in, he pressed each finger to his lips, licking the wine away. Jacqueline watched, spellbound. Then, he slipped her two fingers into his mouth and sucked. It was erotic and sensuous. The simple act ignited her body.

She held her breath as she felt his tongue, strong and powerful, wrap around her fingers and pull. He slipped them in and out repeatedly, licking and savoring all the way to the tip. Then he kissed each finger slowly and deliberately. The man was too good. Seconds later he captured her mouth again. His tongue slipped inside. What he did to her fingers, he did to her tongue. She nearly spasmed as each erotic act drew her in deeper and deeper.

Her arousal soared. All she could think about was his mouth on her, all of her, everywhere. "Tell me," she began breathlessly, "your dream, and then what happened?"

"Then this," he said, turning her around instantly. He slid his arm around her waist and pressed even closer. With their bodies flush, he kissed her lips several times, then he ravished her mouth with purpose and intent. In an instant, their passion was released. He bent low, down the length of her body, showered kisses all over her. Her stomach, her hips, her thighs, her legs, everywhere tingled with delight. Breathless, she placed her hand on his shoulders. "Gregory," she said.

He stood, lifted her up and sat her on the counter, then stepped in between her legs. She pulled his T-shirt up over his head. The perfection of his body nearly took her breath away. She ran her palms over his shoulders and bare chest, feeling the deep ridges from his muscles and abs. She felt her way down his arms as they circled and embraced her. Tightly knotted muscles flexed and relaxed as she readily explored. Her hands trembled as she continued down to the waistband of his jeans. She undid the metal button. Then, steadying her hands, she roamed down against the outside front of his jeans.

She instantly felt the thick fullness of his erection. She licked her lips as her breath caught, knowing this was for her.

All she could think about now was having him inside of her, pressing their bodies together over and over again. She was dizzy with anticipation. She looked into his dark eyes. He'd been watching her as she touched him. The boldness of her actions and him staring prompted her even more. She grabbed the hem of her T-shirt and pulled it up over her head.

After tossing it, she looked at Gregory. His eyes were riveted to her black lace bra. He seemed almost hypnotized by its intricate design. He didn't move or speak. He just stared in seemingly awestruck admiration. Then, slowly, the side of his mouth tipped up ever so slightly. She nearly missed seeing the tiny sign of pleasure. Any hesitation she had instantly vanished.

"See something you like?" she asked teasingly. He nodded slowly, then leaned in and tenderly kissed the sweet budding swell between her breasts. She watched each playful nuzzle. She braced her hands back as he continued kissing and caressing her there. When he licked her, she shuddered. When he nibbled her, she shivered. Then when he sucked her through the lace, she gasped in ecstasy. Her insides gelled as he held her and indulged in her bountiful offering.

He felt so good. She held onto his broad shoulders and arched her chest forward, giving him all of herself. Now the once slow torturous seduction turned to full oral consumption. Without removing the scant fabric, he devoured each tantalizing nipple, making it harden with enthusiastic delight.

Afterward he leaned back, stroked the sides of her

breasts and traced the outline of the bra to the front. When he came to the front clasp, he unsnapped it. The bra popped open, but the lace covering remained mostly in place. Each time she breathed the lace moved just slightly. His finger traced the rounded outline of each tasty orb.

"Gregory," she muttered through his torturous delight, "let's go to my bedroom."

If he heard her, he didn't respond. He opened and pushed the bra aside, freeing her completely. Pert and taunt, each luscious chocolate morsel stood out to him. He captured one breast in his mouth, teasing the already-hardened nipple with his tongue. She shivered as her insides trembled. She closed her eyes and spread her arms wide. This was just like the dream she had the first night. Then all of a sudden he stopped and looked up at her. His eyes narrowed. Then he nodded. He finally heard her.

She sat up. He helped her slide down from the counter. She took his hand and led him to her bedroom, then guided him to stand beside her bed. Biting her lower lip, she assessed her newfound bravado. Then, with steady hands she touched him, letting her hands roam over his bare chest. He was exquisite. Each exceptionally toned muscle tensed beneath her hands. Touching and feeling him gave her a sense of power and control. She liked it. With the front snap already undone, she slowly began unzipping his jeans. The back of her hand brushed against his fullness. She felt his stomach quiver and his arousal grow.

She leaned up, wrapped her arms around his neck to kiss him. Their mouths opened just inches apart. Their breaths mingled, but neither crossed the invisible barrier to touch. Her heart thundered with impatience. Standing here this close was racking her nerves and singeing every part of her body. She held tighter and brought his mouth down to hers. Their lips touched, and there was an instant explosion of passion.

The urgency of their hunger was making him lose control. He tightened his hold on her body and nearly devoured her whole. She slipped her hand between their bodies to end the kiss. "Gregory," she uttered breathlessly, "wait."

He leaned back, closing his eyes a moment to regain the last vestige of diminishing control. His tight hold on her body slackened. He swallowed hard, then took a deep breath.

"Gregory," she repeated, touching his arm.

He opened his eyes. She was staring at him. Her eyes sparkled and shined. He stroked her face gently. "Yes."

"Can we take it slow? It's been a while for me."

"Yes, we can do whatever you'd like. You lead, I'll follow," he promised. She nodded.

Slow was going to be a challenge. He didn't remember ever wanting a woman as much as he wanted her right now. But he intended to wait for as long as she wanted. He knew his pleasure would come. He wanted to see her experience her pleasure first. But right now, it was her move. He watched as she walked to the nightstand, opened the bottom drawer and pulled out a condom. She tossed it on the bed. He walked over and picked it up, then turned to her. "Do you have more?" he asked. She smiled and nodded. "Good," he said.

She grabbed one more and handed it to him. Then she touched the waistband of his jeans and looked up at him. "Take them off," she said. He obeyed dutifully, dropping his jeans to the floor and tossing them aside. She looked down and half smiled. "Everything," she instructed. He complied eagerly.

She looked down the length of his naked body. *Magnificent* wasn't the word. He was glorious. Jacqueline unbuttoned and unzipped her jeans. Greg helped her ease them down her legs, and she tossed them aside. Seeing her standing there in just her lace panties was nearly his undoing. But he held tight to his promise. "Sit down," she said. He did.

She moved to stand between his long legs. He looked up and down the length of her body. She was stunning. He reached up and caressed her neck and shoulders. "Jacqueline, do you have any idea how much I want you right now?" His voice was low, deep and husky. He felt his insides rage with desire.

She looked down at his protruding passion and smiled. "I think I have some idea," she joked.

"Woman, you're killing me," he said, his voice husky and thick with tense emotion.

"Not my intention," she whispered softly, as she climbed onto the bed and motioned for him to join her. She removed her panties. He watched. "Come here." He rolled back to lie beside her. "Come inside," she mouthed. He covered himself then moved on top of her. He spared a moment to look down the lush sensuousness of her succulent body. A shiver of delight streaked through him. She was more than ready for him. Slowly he eased himself up and into her tightness. "More," she muttered. He pressed himself into her body farther. "More, I want all of you," she gasped. She raised her hips, giving him even more access. His heart raced as he delved all the way into her. Her nails bit into his shoulders. Her body was ready to explode.

He filled her completely, and the thick fullness of his body gave her unimaginable pleasure. He began to move his hips. The cadence was slow and easy. Their rhythm synced instantly. It was as if their bodies had been together making love since time began. She raised her hips higher, eager to give as much as he gave. Deeper and deeper he pressed into her. Still hungry for more, she began to move her hips faster, quickening their pace.

He followed her lead. Each push took them closer and closer to their pleasure. Again and again he thrust into her, and she met him with equal vigor. The building wave of frenzied tension grew. The rapture of ecstasy was coming. In and out, ever surging, ever lunging forward, they moved with fierce intent. She shrieked over and over again, enthralled by the coming.

Then, in a blinding light, they came, plunging into that pleasure place together. They stiffened and tensed as the climax engulfed them. Their bodies shook in a massive spasm of pure, rapturous ecstasy. She closed her eyes trembling, totally and completely sated.

Greg leaned down and kissed her. "Are you okay?" he asked.

"Are you kidding?" she said. "I can't stop shaking inside."

He sat up instantly. She opened her eyes, seeing his concern. She smiled. "No, no, I'm fine. I'm more than fine. I've never felt this fine in my life."

He smiled and lay down beside her, pulling her into his embrace. "You had me worried."

"You were right. You do have many skills. And I have a lot more condoms."

"Good, I think we're gonna need every one of them."

"Tonight?" she asked.

"Tonight sounds good."

She chuckled. "And what about tomorrow? We have to go to work and act like none of this ever happened. Can we do that?"

"I don't know, seeing as how every time I look at you, I want you more than ever. But if you want to keep this separate, we can. But right now, I need to taste you again." He kissed her neck and shoulders. She giggled as he kissed down the length of her naked body. She closed her eyes and gasped, enjoying him all over again.

Chapter 13

Cloud nine was nowhere near where Jacqueline's feet touched down today. She was flying high all morning. She left the house early. Gregory's car was already gone. True to his word and her request, they made slow love all night long. Just before dawn he woke her up to tell her he had to go. She barely remembered her response. He was touching her, she remembered that. He had touched her all night. She was right: his hands and his mouth were both lethal. They'd make love then drift off to sleep, then he'd awaken her and they'd make love all over again. They had used the two condoms she'd pulled out and then grabbed a third. He was ravenous and she was insatiable.

It was insane. She'd never felt so completely in control yet still so off balance. Between their lovemaking, they talked and laughed and held each other. No one had ever made her feel so desired. But that was yesterday and last night. This was work and they promised they could do this.

Gregory was out all day as usual. Rumors around the office said that cuts would be getting more drastic and layoffs were imminent. Jacqueline was headed out for the day. She bumped into Greg coming in. "Hi," he said, surprised to see her still there.

"Hi," she said.

"Working late?" he asked.

At her nod, he continued. "I'm glad you're still here. I have to drop a few things off and pick up a file. I wanted to talk to you."

"About what?" she asked.

"Are you headed out?"

"Yes," she said. "What do you want to talk about?"

"Do you want to stop and get something to eat? I'd like to talk to you about the scholarship awards."

Her heart sank, and an ice-cold chill swept over her body. "Please don't tell me you've decided to cut them completely. We've already had the ceremony and gave out promissory notes."

"No, I just had a few quick thoughts about it. We can discuss this over dinner, if that's okay."

She hesitated a brief instant, seeing his expression. He was concerned about something. "What's wrong? What's going on?"

"Dinner?"

"Sure, of course." They chose Chinese food and decided to stop at a restaurant she recommended. They both drove and found parking spaces right next to each other. As they walked the short block to the restaurant, Greg looked in the storefront windows they passed. "I'm still having a hard time getting used to things around here. In New York and D.C., when you want Chinese food you head to Chinatown. In D.C., it's down the street from the Verizon Center. There's a massive arc on H Street Northwest. Within a two-block radius you can find any type of Asian cuisine: Mandarin, Szechuan, Korean, Taiwanese, Malaysian, Vietnamese, Mongolian or Thai."

"We're not exactly living in the Middle Ages here. We have all that, too—it's just more creatively located. For instance you can get most of those cuisines right here in just one place." She stopped at the restaurant's painted window.

"Asian Bistro," he said, reading the sign. "I don't know, looks kind of suspect to me, one place with all kinds of food."

"Trust me, you'll love it."

They went inside. It was exquisitely decorated in traditional Asian motif. There were large, stately bonsai trees, elegant tissue-thin wall hangings, a stunning water fountain and lush, green foliage with floor-to-ceiling rubber and bamboo trees. They were greeted by the hostess and escorted to a secluded booth in the back.

"Not bad," he said, nodding his approval.

The waiter came instantly with a pot of steaming-hot tea. He gave them menus and disappeared as quickly and quietly as he had arrived. Jacqueline watched as Gregory read through the menu. He nodded, obviously impressed by the extent of dishes offered. When the waiter returned, they ordered. "Not bad at all," he affirmed.

"Good. Now, what did you want to talk about?"

"The scholarship awards. We are keeping them. We

have a choice. We can award on a sliding scale of merit or across the board with each recipient receiving three hundred dollars."

Jacqueline exhaled, obviously crestfallen. She had assumed it was on the cutting block as well, but this was just as bad. She shook her head. "But it's a one-thousand-dollar scholarship award. Three hundred dollars is nothing for colleges these days. It's barely the cost of one book."

"That's the best we can do."

She shook her head. "There was no excess. Everything for the event was essential. It was a sit-down luncheon at the hotel and the program was set. It's the same program the city's done for the past twenty years. Gregory, these are exceptional students who've worked hard and gotten extremely high grades in school. We need to recognize that. The awards program was meant to congratulate and appreciate them. The actual scholarship is to encourage them. Remember, these kids will be the ones taking over for us in about twenty years. A lot of them don't have the finances to continue in higher education. These scholarships are a godsend in most cases."

He nodded, seeing the heartfelt earnest. "I have another idea but no promises."

"Thank you. Anything the city can do is appreciated."

"I'm thinking more on the line of private endowment," he said. "I know a few people who give philanthropically. Now, about the other events on the schedule, there's nothing much I can do. Two of them have got to go."

"What about if one goes and two combine?"

"What do you mean?"

Just then their meal arrived. They began eating. Greg

remarked on how surprisingly delicious his meal was. After they'd eaten a few minutes, they got back to the discussion. "Okay, what I was thinking was changing the hot air balloon festival, which is usually a day event and at the beginning of the race, to a night glow at the end. We can have it as the culmination of the mayor's New Year's celebration."

"What exactly is a night glow?"

"It's when hot air balloons are blown up, but don't rise far. It's basically brilliantly colored balloons alight against the night sky to synchronized music."

"I thought once they were blown up, they went up."

"No, not necessarily, and a night glow would really be a wonderful celebration for the start of the New Year. We wouldn't have to change too many things."

"You're gonna have to give me more on this. But if it brings the cost down, and I mean way down, I'll accept it."

She nodded. "It should, and it will definitely be memorable."

Greg nodded. "Okay. It sounds good. Rework the costs and factor in the new ideas."

"The only problems I foresee are the contracts I've already signed."

"Get me the contracts and I'll look them over. I'm sure we can work them through. Good job. That was very creative, combining the two events." He raised his tiny teacup to her. "Congratulations."

Jacqueline raised her cup and clinked his, repeating his toast. After they sipped the tea she set her cup down. "Thank you."

"Don't thank me yet. You have a lot of work to do."

"No problem. Actually, I've already started making arrangements."

"You should really consider having your own business."

"Now what fun would that be?"

"The scholarship, it's personal for you, isn't it?"

"Yes, it is," she admitted. "I was one of those kids a long time ago. The mayor's scholarships changed my life."

"Then I guess we have a responsibility to keep them going."

"I agree, we do. So," she said, changing the subject, "tell me about you, your family."

"Oh, now that's a huge topic."

"What do you mean?"

"Well, you've actually already met my mother."

She frowned. "Your mother? When?"

"Meredith. She is my mother."

Jacqueline's jaw dropped. "Are you serious? She's your mom? She looks so young."

He chuckled. "She works very hard to look that way. She'd appreciate your comments. She's an interior designer."

"What about your dad?"

"My dad was an attorney in New York like my grandfather. He was the youngest partner in a very prestigious law firm in Manhattan. He died at forty of a heart attack while sitting at his desk. He was there all day, and nobody realized it. He was always at his desk, so they just figured he was resting. He was my age now when he had his first heart attack."

"I'm so sorry. That's scary."

"Yes, it is. I was headed down that same path up until a year ago."

"I'm glad you changed."

"Me, too."

"So, brothers and sisters?"

He nodded. "I have two brothers."

"Married, single?"

"Both are single."

"Three eligible bachelors, how does that even happen?"

"I get that question a lot." He finished his last bite.

The waiter came almost instantly and removed their dishes. Moments later he returned with a check and two fortune cookies. Greg paid the bill and moved the saucer of cookies in front of her. Jacqueline took the closest cookie to her. He took the other.

He removed the plastic wrap and broke the cookie open. Then he pulled out the tiny white slip of paper and read the fortune. He smiled. "Hmm, now that's intriguing."

Jacqueline watched curiously. "What does it say?"

He glanced up at her. "Open yours."

She shook her head. "I hate these things. Mine always says something completely weird."

"No stalling, come on, open it."

She ripped the plastic and broke the cookie. Then she pulled out the fortune and read it. She chuckled, looked at him and shook her head.

"What's it say?" he asked.

Her cheeks burned. "No way," she said, shaking her head repeatedly, "no way." She folded the tiny paper and dropped it in her purse. "No one sees that."

He laughed. "Come on, let's go home."

They left and drove home in their own cars. They parked and headed up the path to their condos, talking about plans for the following day. When they got to the vestibule, Jacqueline stopped and turned to him. "Look, I know with these cuts it's a tough position to be put in. I know it's not you. You're just the messenger."

"I'll remember you said that."

"It's just that I worked so hard to get some of these events off the ground."

"Including the hot air balloon festival," he joked.

"Yeah, including that," she said, smiling. "Gregory, you asked me a question a while back. The answer is no, it wouldn't have changed what happened between us before."

Greg smiled happily. "I'm glad to hear that." He reached out and pulled her into his arms. Without hesitation he leaned in and kissed her. "I have been waiting to do that all day long."

She smiled. "Oh, really?"

He nodded. "Yes, really."

Jacqueline caught a black flash out of the corner of her eye. She looked quickly. "Whoa," she said, then pointed. "Oh my God, did you see that?"

"See what?" he asked, turning and looking in the direction she pointed.

"There, that's it. It's that black cat. The one I was telling you about the other night. See him?"

Greg chuckled, amused by her excited angst. "Yes, I see him. That's a new buddy of mine." He bent down and clicked his tongue. The cat shyly crept out from the shadows and slowly moseyed over to him. It rubbed his back up against his leg then placed its paw on his open palm.

"Wait, what are you doing?" she asked, looking at Greg. Then, in one seamless motion, the cat leaped into Greg's arms. He stood up, holding the calm and complacent feline. It purred and dipped its head to rest on his arm.

"That's your cat?" she asked.

"No, but he's been hanging around here lately. I noticed him the other day after the accident. He doesn't have a collar or a tag, so I thought I'd let him stick around for a while."

"You're kidding, right? You're taking in a black cat?"

"I'm taking care of a new friend who brought us together. I'd say I owe him one. He's brought me good luck." Greg scratched the cat's fur behind each ear. The cat nuzzled even closer while purring contentedly. "He's beautiful, isn't he? He's like a miniature black panther."

Jacqueline cautiously kept her distance. She watched as the cat, as black as midnight, slowly closed and opened its eyes and seemed to ease into an even more relaxed position in Greg's arms. He gently stroked his high-gloss, inklike fur. "He's very affectionate and apparently loves attention. I don't know what breed he is, but he's fascinating to watch."

Jacqueline gazed at two glowing, golden eyes staring at her. "I think it's an American Bombay," she said.

Greg looked at her curiously. "How do you know that?"

"Because of its golden eyes and short jet-black sleek fur," she said. "My mother had a black cat just like it when we were growing up. Its name was Patent."

"Patent," Greg repeated. "That's an odd name."

"My mom called it that because she said the cat was her patent-leather accessory. It was always by her side. I remember it even slept with her. She always told us Patent was good luck. I believed her. Then that Friday she died. I never saw the cat again."

"I'm sorry," he said.

She shrugged. "That was a long time ago."

"But it still hurts."

"Not as much as it used to."

"Do you want to pet him?"

"No thanks," she said instantly, and eased closer to the rail leading up to her condo. "I can't believe you're standing there with a black cat." She shook her head in amazement. "It's a stray."

"So am I," he said.

"You know what I mean."

"I'm thinking about calling him Lucky. What do you think?"

She was just about to respond when a car's lights flashed. The cat instantly jumped down and dashed into the shadows.

"Looks like we have company," Greg said, then looked at her as the car parked and the engine shut off. "A friend?"

Jacqueline recognized the car instantly. "It's my sister," she said. "I was supposed to call her tonight."

Greg smiled as Tasha got out of the car and walked over to them. He noticed right away they favored each other. He could also tell her sister wasn't as guarded or hesitant. She smiled openly as she approached. "Hi, Jac," she said, then turned to Greg and smiled. "Hi."

"Tasha, this is Gregory Armstrong. He has the condo

here below me, and he also works with me at the mayor's office. Gregory, this is my sister, Tasha."

"Hello, Tasha," Greg said, smiling. "It's nice to meet you."

Tasha smiled even brighter. "So you're Greg. Wow, you *are* hot."

"Tasha," Jacqueline said quickly, hoping to stop her sister before she really got started. Greg laughed.

"Sorry," Tasha said, smiling playfully. "Greg, nice to meet you, I've heard a lot about you."

"Have you?" Greg looked at Jacqueline and smiled, thinking she'd told her sister about them.

Jacqueline quickly clarified. "Gregory, Tasha and Bethany are good friends. They talk a lot, too much."

"Bethany at the mayor's office?" he asked. Jacqueline nodded. "Well, thank you for the compliment, Tasha. I'll make sure to pass on my thanks to Bethany, as well."

"Oh, who's that?" Tasha asked, seeing the cat come out and wrap around Greg's legs shyly. She bent down and slapped her knees. The cat eased over and looked up. "Hey, Jac, you know this cat looks just like Patent."

"Yes, I know."

"Is he yours?" Tasha asked.

"Actually, I'm thinking about adopting him. I just have to figure out how to go about it."

"Bethany can help with that. She used to work at an animal shelter for a while. What are you gonna call him?"

"Lucky," he said.

"Lucky," she repeated. "I like it, kind of an oxymoron thing, since he's a black cat, right?"

"Actually, it's because he brought your sister and me together. He apparently ran out into the street and, while trying to avoid hitting him, Jacqueline ran into the back of my car."

"Is that your car on the other side?" she asked. He nodded. "The black Jaguar?" He nodded again. Tasha laughed. "That's so funny. Jac, you get it? You avoided a black cat and hit a black Jag. That's funny."

"Yeah, I get it, not so funny. Come on, let's go up. It's getting late. Gregory, thanks again for dinner and for helping with the scholarship event."

"No problem. We'll finish it up tomorrow. I have a few other ideas about the other events."

"Great, we'll talk. Good night," Jacqueline said.

"Nice meeting you, Greg," Tasha said.

"You too, Tasha, I'll make sure to speak with Bethany about Lucky. Good night."

Greg walked into his condo as the sisters went upstairs. Lucky immediately jumped down from his arms and started roaming around. Greg went into the kitchen and grabbed some cream from the refrigerator. He poured some into a saucer and walked back to the living room. Lucky had curled up on the heated marble in front of the fireplace. Greg set the dish down and watched as Lucky walked over and began lapping up the cream.

Greg smiled and sat down. He'd been thinking about the conversation he had with Carter a few days ago. Although he'd been only joking with Jacqueline about their fate, maybe there was something to this keeper thing. He glanced up at the ceiling. Being with Jacqueline these past few days had made him realize how much he wanted her in his life. From the first instant he saw her, she was all he seemed to think about.

He had fallen for her in just a matter of days. He knew it was too fast, but he couldn't help himself. The instant he saw her, she became a part of him. Yes, he hardly knew her, but he didn't care. He knew her spirit. It lived within him now. Everything in his heart told him she was the woman he'd been looking for all his life.

Lucky moseyed over, curled around his legs and then jumped up onto the sofa beside him. Greg stroked the cat's black fur then scratched its ears. The cat looked up at him. Greg smiled. "How did you know she was the one?" he asked rhetorically. Lucky purred, closed his eyes and lay his head on Greg's lap.

Greg rested his head back and marveled at how his life had changed in less than a year. He's gone from being a dangerously excessive workaholic with high blood pressure, high cholesterol and maxed-out stress levels to a healthy, relaxed man with a bright future and in love with a beautiful woman.

The scare of his father's death, and his doctor's dire warnings, had straightened him out almost instantly. He was thirty-two. The same age his father was when he had his first heart attack. He knew he was on his way to following in his footsteps and doing the exact same thing. His father died at forty, leaving a young wife and three sons to mourn him. Well, he intended to be around when his own sons grew up. He smiled, thinking about having sons with Jacqueline. He liked the sound of it.

Chapter 14

"OMG—talk about yummy-licious," Tasha began, as soon as she closed the door behind her. "Bethany was right—he *is* gorgeous. And girl, you acting like you don't know, please. You'd better jump on that."

"He's not a bicycle, Tasha."

"Doesn't mean you can't still ride," Tasha quipped. She sashayed straight to the kitchen and grabbed a bottle of water. Jacqueline followed while flipping through her mail. Tasha held her water, then rummaged through the refrigerator for anything interesting. Jacqueline tossed some junk mail in the trash, and leaned back on the counter across from where she and Gregory had been just the night before. Her heart tumbled and quivered. Tasha closed the refrigerator door, turned and smiled. "You know he likes you, don't you? I mean *really* likes you."

"What makes you say that?"

"Good Lord, are you kidding? The man damn near glows when he's looking at you. Seriously, his eyes like glaze over. Jason's squinty eyes never did that. Bethany told me that he kept staring at you at the reception the other night." She went over to the alcove and sat down at the table. "Do you like him?"

Jacqueline sat down across from her. "Yes, I like him. I like him too much. It's crazy, I know. I don't even know him."

"It's not crazy. It's wonderful. It's like love at first sight." Jacqueline didn't respond. "Hey, what's wrong?"

"I told him about Mom and Dad. I can't believe I did that."

"Jac, the perfect man doesn't come along every day. You pour your heart out to him. That has to mean something, don't you think?"

"I don't know what it means. Maybe he's just a good listener."

"Or maybe inside you know there's more."

"There can't be more. He's leaving."

"Where's he going?"

"I don't know. Back to D.C., I guess."

"Go with him."

"Yeah, right," Jacqueline said with a smirk.

"Why not?"

"Because I have a job, and a condo—"

"Both of which you can find in D.C."

Jacqueline looked at her sister and just shook her head. "I don't know what it is. The moment I see him I feel connected, like I've known him forever. I talk and open up and tell him things about myself that I've never told anyone. Not even you. I can't help myself. We were sitting on the swings in the playground and I just—"

"Wait. He took you to a playground, and you actually went? Ah, man, this is so perfect. Do you know how remarkable that is?"

"I'm not that bad, am I?"

Tasha nodded, laughing. "Yes, you are, and you know it. So, tell me, did you get a chance to kiss him yet?"

"Yes, we kissed the first night," Jacqueline confessed giddily. "I still can't believe I did that. I'd just met him and there I was in his bedroom, kissing him and feeling—"

"Whoa. What? You were where?" Tasha said, giggling.

"In his bedroom, and no, it's not what you think. He was giving me a T-shirt to wear that first night when I got locked out. I don't know how we got onto the subject of being spontaneous. Then I just walked over and kissed him."

"Oh man. This is so cool. It's like right out of the movies. Don't you see? It's like destiny is throwing you together. It's like Love at First Sight 101."

Jacqueline laughed. "Tasha, you're such a romantic dreamer."

"I might be a dreamer, but you're falling for him."

"I just met him."

"Jac, don't you see, it's not about time. It's about what you feel inside. It's the connection. You feel it, don't you? I know he does. You can see it in his eyes. It's like something drawing the two of you together."

"I don't believe in fate and destiny."

"I don't think that really matters. When the universe speaks, that's it. Destiny believes in you."

Jacqueline shook her head. "You're forever into your 'metaphysical nature of the universe' stuff. Everything isn't that perfect and simple, Tasha."

"Love is," she said. "When you meet the one person you're supposed to be with, you know it." She nodded while eyeing her sister. "I think you just met him. So, when are you gonna seal the deal?"

"Seal the deal?" Jacqueline asked. Then it hit her a second later, and she opened her mouth in surprise. "Tasha," she said, grinning and blushing, "I can't believe you just asked me that. It's none of your business."

Tasha looked at her sister as she blushed. She gasped, then started laughing. "Oh my God, you already did, didn't you? When, the first night?" she asked with a wide smile.

Jacqueline looked at her sister in shock. "I don't know how you guessed that."

"Please, girl, it's all over your face. You're glowing just like him. I wondered what that was when I walked up and saw you two together. It's like Bethany said. He was eating you up with his eyes at the reception and then again at some meeting you had."

"What meeting?" she asked.

"Skip that. Go back to the details. When? How was it?"

"I am not sitting here giving you details," Jacqueline said. She stood up and went to the refrigerator. She pulled out a bottle of water, unsnapped it and took a long sip. "But no, it wasn't the first night."

Tasha turned, smiled and nodded approvingly. "I'm happy for you, Jac. I really am. It's about time you found your heart."

"Thanks," Jacqueline said, then hugged Tasha. "How's Dad?"

Tasha smiled, happy her sister asked. "He's good, he's very different than before. I wish you could talk to him. His voice is strong and he sounds so encouraged. I've never heard that in his voice before. He wants to talk to you."

"I don't think we have anything to say to each other anymore. It's been two years."

"Just talk to him. You'll see."

"I'll think about it."

"He needs us now, like we needed him all those years ago. I keep thinking what Mom might want. I don't remember her as well as you do, but I don't think she'd want us to turn our backs on him."

"You're right, she wouldn't," Jacqueline said. She realized for the first time that Tasha was a lot more like their mother than she ever gave her credit for. Their mother was compassionate, with a huge, giving heart. She was also quick to give and forgive. That was why she and her dad stayed together for so long, even though he had disappointed her repeatedly. "You're a lot like Mom."

"I am," Tasha said, smiling brightly, "really, I wish I remembered more about her."

"I remember this one time we were out shopping. There was this little girl begging her mom for the same doll Mom had just bought you. I guess they couldn't afford it. Anyway, Mom bought it for her. I don't know who was happier, the little girl or Mom." Jacqueline paused, then nodded. "I'll tell you what, I'll think about talking to Dad."

Tasha nodded. "Good, that's all I hoped for. Okay,

I gotta go. It's getting late. I'll talk to you later about what to bring for Christmas dinner. Bye."

Thankfully, the rest of the evening was blissfully quiet. Jacqueline decided to stay in and detail more of the ideas she had told Greg about. An hour later, she was pleased with what she'd come up with. The balloon festival coinciding with the city's New Year's celebration was a wonderful idea. It was perfect. She packed everything away, then grabbed a quick shower and slipped into her sweats.

It was late, but she was feeling restless. She stepped out onto the balcony to get some air. The night sky sparkled and shined with tiny, brilliant stars. The almost full moon was radiant as it illuminated the pristine grounds. She watched a plane soar across the sky. She thought about the hot air balloon festival. It was one of the happiest memories she had as a child. The festival wasn't the biggest or the most elaborate, but it was the most memorable for her. Hundreds and hundreds of balloons filled the sky. They always brought a crowd to the area. Hopefully this year would be even better.

She felt a sudden sadness as a slight chill hung in the air. She thought about her father and hoped he'd truly changed. He'd gotten worse after her mother was killed. She knew he always blamed himself. She wrapped her arms around herself and looked down. Gregory had come outside. "Hello," she called out, getting his attention.

He turned, looked up and smiled. "Hey," he said. "I guess you couldn't sleep either."

She shook her head. "Too excited and too much to think about," she said.

He nodded. "Me, too," he said, smiling. "You look

beautiful up there. I'd recite the balcony scene from *Romeo and Juliet,* but I have no idea how it goes."

She laughed. "That's okay. Why don't I just come down for a minute?"

"Good idea."

She went over to the steps leading down to the patio area. As she came down, Gregory walked over and met her at the bottom step. He smiled as she approached. "You look sensational."

"In simple sweatpants and a jacket?" she asked.

"In anything, in nothing," he said, as he took her hand and tucked it under his arm. Neither spoke as they strolled farther down onto the grassy yard. They both looked up at the night sky. The moon was luminous and the stars seemed radiant. "It's so peaceful and open here. It's like you can see every star and every planet in the universe."

She looked at him and smiled. She got the sense that Paradise was quickly growing on him. "I guess with the tall buildings and city lights you can't see the sky much."

"True, you have to get out of the city to see a night sky like this one. And even then, I doubt you'd see anything as spectacular and magnificent as this."

"Come on, I want to show you something." They cut across the yard and continued to walk down to the small lake behind the house. They stood by the water's edge. The stars' reflections made the still water sparkle. "Watch this." Jacqueline picked up a small stone and tossed it into the water. Ripples appeared as soon as the stone hit the water's surface. With the sky's reflection, it looked as if the sky was waving and moving.

"Wow, that's pretty cool." He picked up a stone and

tossed it in, too. His bounced twice before going in. The ripples were twice as large and even more sensational.

Jacqueline laughed. "Hey, not bad. I like that."

He picked up another stone and tossed it again. They stood watching the water's trembles. It looked almost magical. After a while Jacqueline walked over to sit on the bench and enjoy the peaceful beauty of the moment. Greg sat beside her and draped his arms around her shoulders. She nuzzled close. The setting was dreamy and romantic. "I'm headed out of town next week."

"Spending the holidays with family?" she asked.

"Yes, and I'd like you to come with me."

"Me? What?"

"Of course you, I'd like you to meet my family."

"Gregory, it's too soon. We've been together for only a week. We don't even know where this is going. It could all fall apart and disappear in the next few days. Nothing ever lasts forever."

He turned to her and tipped her chin up to look into her eyes. "Jacqueline, I know exactly where this is going. I didn't intend it and I didn't see it coming. I don't need another few days, weeks or months to know how I feel about you. I've always known. From the instant I saw you on Friday the thirteenth. You're the one, my keeper. I love you."

Her heart beat double time. Her mouth went dry and she could barely speak. "It's been one week."

"No, it's been the beginning of a lifetime, our life together. I've never been so completely sure about anything in my life. When I look at you, I see my future, my destiny. I love you so much."

"Gregory, but what do we do—"

"No concerns, not tonight. Tonight, let's just enjoy

our love. Tomorrow will come soon enough." He stood and reached his hand out. She took it and they walked back to the steps leading up to her condo. He glanced up. "I guess this is good night."

She nodded, then took a step up and turned back to him. They were exactly eye to eye. He placed his hands on her waist and brought her closer. "I'm getting more and more addicted to you." He dipped his head to the bend of her neck and inhaled the sweet softness of her body. He kissed her neck tenderly. Then he buried his face in the softness of her hair. "I do love you."

Jacqueline took a deep breath, relishing the feel of his closeness. She wrapped her arms around his neck and held tight as her body nearly melted right there on the spot. They looked into each other's eyes as the kiss came gently. She pressed her lips to his, then opened to him. Their tongues began an elaborate dance of desire. It was powerful and passionate and consumed every part of their bodies. After a few moments she stepped back breathless. "This is leading to…"

"Yeah, I think it is…." he said.

"Maybe we should…"

"Yes, okay, maybe we should…" He stopped and rested his forehead on her chest between her breasts. He closed his eyes to get a grip on his body's surging need. "I want you so much."

"Hey," she said softly, "that's not what I meant." He looked up at her just as she leaned back and began pulling the zipper down the front of her sweat jacket. She wasn't wearing anything underneath. She'd never intentionally seduced a man before. She had no idea what she was doing, but she knew it was working and she loved every second. Greg's eyes watched as the zipper pulled down. The tender swelling sweetness of her pert breasts peeked through. Greg's mouth went dry. Jacqueline slowly continued unzipping until the jacket was completely open. "Correction—I'm way past addiction."

She leaned in and nibbled his earlobe. "Your place or mine?" she whispered.

"Both," he said.

"I need to lock my door."

"Mine is already locked." He pressed his velvety soft lips to her neck again and then traveled down, nibbling and licking until he found his treasure. He moved closer, trapping her body against the rail. Her heart had never pumped so fast or so hard. His hand inched between their bodies and freely roamed and explored her. He cupped her breasts, then tweaked her nipples, rubbing each in between his thumb and finger. She shuddered inside as they hardened instantly. The stinging pleasure made her gasp. She arched back as he captured her in his mouth. He licked liberally, tantalizing the nipple of each breast with the tip of his tongue.

Jacqueline closed her eyes, reeling in the sweet sensation of his mouth. He was masterful, with a skill she never imagined even existed. He brought both breasts together. She opened her eyes and looked down. The erotic sight made her wet. He licked gently, then began sucking, drawing her into the warmth of his mouth.

He pressed closer still. She nearly lost all senses, feeling the hardness of his erection. They kissed, continuing the erotic foreplay beneath the stars. She reached down and stroked his body, feeling the hard solidity of his chest and stomach. Then she went lower. The kiss deepened. She felt him lift her and begin climbing the stairs. Before she knew it she was in her bedroom lying on her own bed. Gregory was there with her. He removed his shirt. The full, glorious perfection of his chest thrilled her. She sat up and watched as he removed the rest of his clothes.

He was magnificent, and he was full and ready for her. She rolled over, opened the side drawer and grabbed some condoms. But before she rolled back, he was there lying beside her. He began stroking the full length of her body. Touching and kissing everywhere. It reminded her of their first almost-night together when he massaged her to sleep. But this time it was different.

He removed her sweatpants and panties, then began kissing her back. He caressed her shoulders and kissed her up and down. "Roll over," he whispered. She did. He gazed at her and smiled like a little boy in a candy shop. He gently touched her breasts, then the flat of her stomach and finally the sweet entrance of her pleasure. She was already wet and wanting. He pressed his finger inside of her and smiled, and her thighs tightened, gripping his hand. "I like that. Open for me."

She moaned and looked at him in near mindless ecstasy. She opened her legs and he dipped his finger in again. She gasped as he found the tiny nub of her pleasure. Her body trembled as he continued to stroke her. Each stroke was slow and deliberate. She closed her eyes tightly, enraptured by his talent. Her stomach quivered as each madding stroke sent her reeling. Then she felt something different. Her eyes flew open. She saw him. He was between her legs tasting her. Her senses all but shattered.

She closed her eyes tight and tried to hold on, but she couldn't. Each lustful lick and tantalizing taste shot right through her body. She shivered and trembled. Every nerve in her body tingled. He was devouring her. His tongue went deeper and his mouth embraced all of her. She felt the rapture coming. Then he stopped and looked up at her. She opened her eyes and lay breathless. An instant later he dipped his head and her world exploded. She screamed his name over and over again, as each fitful climax erupted, making her cringe and writhe in pleasure.

He grabbed a condom and entered. She screamed his name again. Her nails bit into his shoulders as his hips moved, deepening his penetration. He had filled her, in and out, over and over again, until his body went still and rigid. He stopped. But she could feel that he was still hard inside of her. She pushed him to roll over and got on top. With him still deep inside and rock hard, she impaled herself and rode him hard and long until he went weak. Their bodies shattered and quaked, releasing the last of their control.

"Jacqueline," he muttered, breathless. "I'll never be able to walk away from you."

"Good." She smiled as she cuddled into his embrace. Greg stayed awake awhile longer.

Chapter 15

The next few days passed with business as usual. Just as they promised, they were both completely professional at work. No one had a clue there was anything between them other than coworker friendship. They worked diligently and tirelessly during the day and loved each other at night. His place or her place, they took turns. It became their little secret. But once in a while, when they were in the office late, there'd be a sly smile passing between them. Other than that, they kept themselves entirely businesslike.

When the weekend came they decided to do something special. She suggested they visit the site of the New Year's night glow she was planning. She packed a full lunch and Greg drove. The site was several miles outside the city limits. The land was owned by the city, deeded over sixty years ago. There was always the intent to sell the property, but the city never followed through.

They pulled off the highway onto the side road leading to the open grounds. Two miles farther, they arrived at the flat, sparsely grassed terrain. They stopped, got out and looked around. They were completely alone. There was no breeze, no sound. The placid stillness made it seem as if they were the only people on earth. "Wow, it's beautiful. This really is the desert, isn't it?" Greg asked.

"Yep, more or less. Welcome to the real Arizona," she said. He looked around in amazement. "Actually there are lush parts and desert parts. Tonto National Forest is off in that direction. But mostly it's flat and tan, with incredible skies that go on forever."

"This place is awesome. It's like our own little world. There's not a soul in sight."

"That's probably more true than not. I doubt there's anyone around here for miles."

He playfully pulled her close to his body. "Now, I like the sound of that. We can do anything we want and not be seen."

She laughed. "We wouldn't exactly not be seen. There are all kinds of eyes watching—birds, scorpions, rattlesnakes, spiders, coyotes."

"I don't mind a small audience. What about you?" he joked, as he nibbled her ear.

Jacqueline laughed again. "You're terrible," she said, still wrapped in his arms. "But, I completely agree, it is pretty awesome here. Sometimes I forget the real natural beauty of this place."

"Who owns it?" he asked.

"The land was deeded over to the city about sixty

years ago. The man who owned it left it to Paradise Cove in his will."

"So it's an asset. Could the city sell it?" he asked.

"The man's will has certain stipulations that the city has never been able to rectify. The land is used primarily for events like the night glow or open-air concerts."

She detailed exactly what she had in mind. He loved her vision and ideas. They walked and talked about her plans for the night glow. "It won't take too long to get the balloons ready. I plan to start the main festivities at sunset. I've already lined up the vendors and buses. Everybody knows about the new location. The balloon pilots and their ground teams are excited. We won't have the full hundred and fifty, but we'll have plenty to make an incredible showing."

"How are you going to get them here?" he asked, following as she walked around.

"They have ground crews in vans."

"How exactly do hot air balloons work?"

"Simple science. Hot or heated air rises in cooler air. Pilots heat the air with a propane burner, sending it into the envelope or the balloon. If the air cools they just heat it again. The bigger the flame the higher you go. There's a parachute on top to help control the speed of ascent and descent."

"How do they travel horizontally?"

"Pilots learn to catch wind currents. Some are stronger than others. There's no real steering mechanism involved."

Greg was really impressed with her knowledge of hot air balloons. "How do you know so much about hot air balloons?"

"My dad used to pilot one years ago," she said. "I

guess I picked it up from him. I was always scared to death to be in one. There's no control and no set plan. It's mostly chance and you seldom land where you expect. It's mostly all improvised."

"It sounds a lot like life—up, down, sideways. We take our chances every day. So, your dad did this as a hobby?"

"Yes, he used to love it. But that was when we were a family. He had many skills, none of which included planning, responsibility and dependability."

"I guess that's maybe why you're such a talented planner."

"I never thought of it that way, but yeah, I guess so." She looked far out into the barren region. A bird caught her eye. She watched it soar until it was out of sight.

"So tell me, what happens if things don't go as you plan?" he asked guardedly.

"That only happens on Friday the thirteenth," she joked. "Actually, I just make another plan and go from there."

"You didn't plan on us," he said.

"No, I didn't. Did you?"

"No, but I'm glad destiny stepped in."

"Destiny, huh?" she asked.

"Yes, destiny."

She looked out into the desert again. The sky was crystal clear, with just a single cloud moving lazily across the horizon. "It looks like the perfect day to go up."

Greg watched the cloud with her. "If your dad still does it, maybe he can take us up sometime. Does he still pilot?"

"No, not anymore. That was a very long time ago. We don't speak much anymore."

"You should think about forgiving him. I'm not saying he did his best—he clearly didn't. But your heart is too big and too generous not to. It's not the woman you are, the woman I love, and I can see it's tearing you apart inside. You're blessed to have your father still with you. Sometimes I wish I could talk to my dad. He died when we were kids, so none of us really remember him much, just thoughts and stray moments, that's all. I miss him. Maybe it's time."

Jacqueline didn't reply. She just wrapped her arm around his waist and held tight. They stood staring out, as their memories traveled in all directions. She considered his comment, and she thought about what Tasha said about their father. They were both right. She missed her father, too. She hoped he was better. It had been too long. Maybe it was time to let go of the pain.

"You know, I've never seen a hot air balloon up close. I'm looking forward to this New Year's celebration."

"Good. Then maybe if you're really impressed, you'll let me keep it in the lineup for next year's events," she said, smiling slyly, knowing she was breaking their promise to keep business and personal separate. He didn't smile. He just looked away. She saw his troubled reaction. "Hey, I was joking. Don't look so serious."

"Have you ever thought about opening your own events-planning business?"

"Yeah, sometimes," she said. "I toyed with the idea, but the up-front cost would be exorbitant. Office space, staff, incidentals. Then there's finding clients. I can't afford that, and in this economy banks aren't as friendly as they used to be."

"Maybe the city could be one of your clients."

"Then what's the sense of opening my own business? I already work for the city."

"It would be yours and you could do different types of projects like weddings, private parties and things like that."

She smiled thoughtfully. "That would be nice, doing something different sometimes. I love my job, but not being stifled by city regulations and rules would be great. But, it's not gonna happen."

"It might. I could give you the money."

"A loan? No thanks, I've always heard that loans and lovers don't mix," she said dismissively, then walked out farther and looked around. The truth was, having her own company would be wonderful. It was her dream, but getting money from Gregory would be a mistake. She turned as he walked up beside her. "That looks like a great spot to picnic. Let's eat under the tree over there." He agreed. They grabbed the picnic basket and blanket and walked over to the sole Arizona Sycamore. He spread out the blanket where they sat and ate. Afterward they lay in each other's arms, talking and watching the sun just above the horizon.

"The holidays are next week. I'm leaving Monday night."

She sat up on her elbows and turned to him. "How long will you be away?"

"I'll be back on Christmas. My family has a big celebration the day before. I wish you were coming with me."

"I know, maybe another time. We'll see how it goes. If you get back early maybe you could join me at the house. My sister and some friends are coming over for Christmas dinner."

"Sounds good, I'll try," he said, as she lay back in his arms. "I need a favor."

"What, grab the newspaper? Sure."

"No, I need you to take care of Lucky for me."

She sat up quickly this time, taking him off guard. "Your black cat?" she asked. He nodded and sat up, too. She looked at him, then started laughing. "You're joking, right?"

He shook his head. "No, he needs someone to look out for him. You're perfect."

"I can't," she said, standing up quickly. All she could think about was Lucky running off like Patent did after her mom died.

"Yes, you can," he said knowingly, as he stood.

"You don't understand. I left the door open and my mom's cat, Patent, ran out. It was my fault. I can't. What about a kennel or a pet hotel? They have them, don't they?" she asked.

"Yes, but I'd like you to watch him, please. Nothing will go wrong, I promise you."

She looked up into his eyes. It was such an easy request. All she had to do was let go of her fears. Then, amid a dozen of reasons why she shouldn't, she relented. "What exactly do I have to do?"

He smiled and held her close. She was letting go of her fears and superstitions. "Thank you. You'll be wonderful. I'll tell you everything you need to know."

"You'd better. The last thing I need is a black cat mad at me. I could have bad luck for the rest of my life."

"I have no doubt the two of you will do just fine. Thank you."

Jacqueline shook her head, not knowing what to think. She'd just agreed to cat-sit a black cat, the same one that ran in front of her on Friday the thirteenth. She must be in love.

The sun had just about dipped beyond the far mountains in the west. The massive, open sky lit up in a fiery display of vibrant colors. It was spectacular to see, but they didn't see much of it. They made love beneath the blazing violet-crimson sky. The audience she talked about never showed. It was just them beneath the heavens. Just before complete darkness, they headed home.

When they got back, they stopped at his place to relax the rest of the evening. Greg turned on the fireplace, and they sat in the living room talking and enjoying the cozy warmth of each other's company. "This is the perfect ending to the perfect day," Greg said. Jacqueline nodded and snuggled closer in his embrace. "You know, I was serious about you considering starting your own business. And I didn't say it would be a loan. I said I could give you the money."

She sat up and looked at him. "Exactly how much money do you have?"

"My family is very wealthy," he said casually.

"Millions wealthy or multimillions wealthy?" she questioned.

"Multimillions. My great-grandfather was an engineer and inventor. It started with him. We became the Armstrong family of New York. My grandfather, Thomas Armstrong, was a stockbroker on Wall Street years ago. He did extremely well, too. I grew up with a nanny, live-in housekeepers and cooks. I went to private schools, we vacationed at the family home in Martha's

Vineyard and the Hamptons, and it was nothing to have politicians, CEOs, and TV and film stars at our house just for Saturday lunch. The money's there. It's yours, use it."

She looked at him, stunned. "You're serious, aren't you?"

"Yes, I am."

"But that's your family, that's not you, right?" The whole idea that he came from so much money was staggering. She would never have guessed.

He smiled. "Actually, it's me, too. I have money in my own right, not to mention several trust funds."

"Do you have a private plane?" she half joked.

"No, I don't, but my grandfather does. I'm hitching a ride with him to D.C. I still want you to come with me."

"I can't. I still have so much to do for this year's and next year's events. I've planned a whole new budget-conscious series of events. I think you and the council will be pleased."

"No. Jacqueline," he said almost painfully. "The city's having serious financial difficulties, more so than is generally known. There was gross mismanagement. They had overextended themselves and borrowed against assets they no longer had available. As a result, they need to make major cuts."

"What does all that mean?" she asked, getting more alarmed.

"I shouldn't be, but I'm telling you this before it's released. It means they have to cut a department budget."

"Which department?" she asked, dreading the answer. Her heart pounded like a jackhammer.

He took a deep breath and exhaled slowly. "Jacqueline, the council voted to cut your department budget."

"What?" she said, obviously shocked.

"I'm sorry," he said, seeing her reaction.

"How much of a cut?" she said guardedly. She knew. She just needed him to confirm it.

"All of it." He paused. "They're laying you off."

"Oh my God." She was stunned. The sting of his words staggered her. She stood up and walked away. He followed, grabbing her arm. She shrugged away from him. "How long? When do I have to leave?"

"The first week of January," he said.

"So I'm out of a job in just over one week?" She sat down, shook and lowered her head in shock. "What am I gonna do?"

"Jacqueline, I know you're upset, but—"

She looked up at him fiercely. "Yeah, I'm upset. How long have you known about this?"

"Does it matter?"

She stood. "Yes, it matters to me. How long?" He didn't answer. "Since before we made love?" she asked.

He nodded. "Yes. I was working in Phoenix a week before I got here, before we met. I was hired to cut waste and make the hard decisions. I made the recommendation last week that the city cut—"

"*You* made the recommendation." Suddenly she couldn't breathe. The air in the room felt as if it had been sucked out. "You, knowing how much this job means to me. It's my life. It's all I have. How could you?"

"Jacqueline, it's not about the job and it's not personal."

"Don't," she nearly screamed, holding her hand up to

stop him. "Just don't. I'm so sick of hearing that it's not personal. Well, guess what—it *is* personal, it's *always* personal. *We* were personal. Or was this just part of the master plan, too? I need to get out of here and think. My head is spinning." She grabbed her purse.

"Jacqueline, everything will be all right. Trust me."

"How can you say that? Your world hasn't just fallen apart. Mine has." She walked to his front door and opened it wide. He followed her.

"Jacqueline, please, I know you're scared, but trust me."

She spun around quickly. "Trust you? I already did. Now I don't have a job."

"Jacqueline, I love you."

"Love? This is your love? You just took away the one thing in my life I could always depend on. I trusted you with that and I trusted you with my heart."

"You can't leave like this."

"Watch me," she said, hurrying up the steps to her condo.

"Jacqueline, trust me," he said, following her.

"How can I?" She opened her door and went inside. Greg heard her tears. His heart broke. But he knew she'd be all right even if she didn't right now.

Chapter 16

The start of the Christmas holiday week was pure chaos. The mayor was away on vacation. Bethany and a few others were out, and half the office was already celebrating. Jacqueline was in the office and, thankfully, for her sake, Gregory was gone all morning and afternoon. She spent most of her day alone changing and finalizing arrangements and making new plans for the New Year's celebration. With everything she still had to do, she didn't have time to even plan her next step. She was getting laid off in a week, she had no prospects and knew of no one hiring. For the first time in her life she didn't have the answer.

She thought about the weekend. It had started out so right and then ended so wrong. She knew she had probably overreacted. Ultimately it wasn't exactly Gregory's fault the city had to let her go. But that didn't make it hurt any less. They had barely talked after that. No, correction, *she* had barely talked. After their conversation Friday night, she went home and cried for an hour. He knocked on her door and called her, but she told him she was going to bed. Then she had packed a bag and hung out with her sister the rest of the weekend. Saturday and Sunday breezed by in a flash.

While out Christmas shopping, she told Tasha about her job and what happened with Gregory. Tasha was supportive and told her this was the perfect time to open her own business. She also told her to talk to Gregory. Then of course the conversation had inevitably come up about their father. Tasha wanted to see him. Jacqueline didn't. She wasn't ready yet. They decided to sleep on it and decide Christmas day. She got home late Sunday evening and saw that Greg's car was there. She knew Monday would be tough. There was no avoiding him in the same office. She knew she had to clear the air. She knocked, but didn't get an answer. He was out, probably running.

Monday morning, his car was already gone when she left for work, and he'd been in and out before she got to the office. She worked at a near panic getting the last details together for the next week. When her cell rang, she picked up without looking at the ID. It was her sister. "Hey, Tasha," she said.

"Jac, before you get all twisted upset, I just want you to know that I'm doing this because it's the right thing to do."

"Tasha, I have a million things on my desk. I don't have time for your romantic dramas. So whatever you're about to do, just don't."

"This has nothing to do with me. It's for you. Hold on…"

There was a pause. She waited wondering what her sister was up to now. "Tasha. Tasha. Tasha, I don't have time…"

"Jackie." She heard the voice. Her heart skipped a beat. No one had called her that name in over two years. She didn't even answer to it anymore. "Jackie, are you there?" She took a deep breath, steeling herself against the emotional turmoil she knew would be coming. "Jackie, it's okay, you don't have to say anything. I understand.

"I was never a good father and I don't blame you for not wanting to see me or speak to me. I just want you to know how proud I am of you. Your mother would be proud, too. She loved you girls so much. I do, too. I know I never showed it. I left you all alone. What kind of father does that? There are no words to express how sorry I am. I was selfish and stupid. I spent my life trying to catch the brass ring, not realizing I already had it in my family, you girls."

Jacqueline's eyes watered as tears threatened to fall. "Hi, Dad," she finally said, softly. Her voice was thick with feeling and emotion. A lifetime of harsh memories came flooding to her, then seemed to fade away. Gregory was right; she had to forgive him. Love wouldn't allow her to do anything else.

"It's good to hear your voice, Jackie. I can't talk long. Your sister's here with me and she's beautiful. You both are doing a great job taking care of each other."

"Dad, I'm sorry about everything."

"There's nothing to be sorry about. None of this is your fault. It's mine. I messed up. No excuses. I went too far trying to get my life back together. Blind desperation can make a man do things he never thought he'd do. I wanted my life back, and it never occurred to me that I already had everything in the world I needed in you and your sister. I know now that I need to turn my life around. I've disappointed you over and over again."

"Yes, you have." Her words nearly stuck in her throat.

"I'm not asking for another chance or for your forgiveness. I know I don't deserve it."

"No, you don't. But you get it anyway," she said tearfully. "Love forgives."

"Thank you, sweetheart," he said. She could hear the heaviness in his voice as he spoke. "I love you. Here's your sister back."

"Hey, it's me again. I know you gotta go, but..." Tasha said.

"Tasha, thanks."

"You're welcome. I'll see you on Christmas."

She pressed the end button on her cell, then sat just holding the phone for a while. She didn't expect to hear his voice, but she was glad she did. Tasha was right; he did sound different. A warm, centering feeling swept over her. Making peace with her father made her feel good. He was a man with troubles, and she hoped that someday he'd truly get his life back together and stop chasing what he already had. After a few minutes more, she went back to work, more devoted and dedicated than ever.

Greg came back to the office late that afternoon. As soon as he walked in, Jacqueline looked up. "Hello, Jacqueline," he said, happy to see her.

"Hi, Gregory," she said softly, looking up from her desk.

"I'm glad you're here," he said, as he walked to his desk while reviewing his PDA. "I just got final approval for the New Year's celebration. The money is there. It seems quite a few council members are very excited about your idea. Congratulations. Some are actually looking forward to going."

"Good. They'll have a good time."

He sat and swiveled his chair to face her. "I think the fact that the governor will be in attendance changed a few minds. I'm impressed—that was a brilliant move, inviting him. Quite a few people took notice."

"That wasn't the intent, but I'm glad they did."

"Also, Jacqueline—"

"Gregory, wait," she said standing. "I have a meeting off-site in a few minutes. So before we talk about business again, I'd like to talk about what happened between us the other night."

"Sure," he said, just as his office phone rang. "I need to get this. I'm expecting a call from Phoenix." She nodded. He picked up, but it wasn't the call he was expecting.

"Greg, it's Paul Jenkins at the Department."

Greg was surprised to hear his old boss's voice. "Paul, hey, how are you? Happy holidays." He glanced over at Jacqueline, seeing that she'd sat down and gone back to work.

"You, too. I'm doing well, how are you? That's the question."

"Fine, I've never felt better. The time off has been wonderful."

"Excellent, I'm glad to hear that," Paul said encouragingly. "So are you ready to get back into the thick of things here in D.C.?"

"I'm always ready. So, what can I do for you, Paul?"

"I think it's what I can do for you. You expressed an interest in coming back to the Department when you left, and I just might have something for you. An interesting position crossed my desk. I thought of you immediately. It's not in the system yet, so I pulled it to give you first crack. But I'm gonna need an answer from you as soon as possible. There's an opening here in the Department as legal liaison to the Pentagon. I think you're perfect for it. As a matter of fact I've already talked to OPM about getting you additional and elevated clearance. With your performance record, they don't see a problem, so we're good to go. There'll be a very nice bump in pay and a few other perks. So, what do you think? Interested?"

Greg smiled happily. This was exactly what he was looking for. "Are you kidding? It sounds incredibly tempting," he said, glancing over at Jacqueline. She had gathered her things. She waved and hurried out the door to her meeting.

"Excellent. But know that I can't hold this for long."

"I understand."

"Why don't you stop by the office in the next few days and we'll talk?"

"Actually, Paul, I'm in Arizona right now. I have a flight out this evening. I'll be stopping in D.C. tonight, and then continuing to New York tomorrow."

"Sounds good. When you get to D.C., give me a call. We'll set something up. This position is custom-made for you, Greg. The hours are long, there's a lot of travel, but I see good things. I'm not going to snow you, it's high-stress and difficult, and it's a career opportunity of a lifetime. I'll see you tomorrow."

"Sounds good. I'll see you tomorrow, Paul." He ended the call and sat at his desk, pondering his conversation with his friend. This was his chance to go back to D.C. and do what he enjoyed. It also meant that he needed to talk to Jacqueline about going with him. That, he knew, wouldn't be easy. But since her department and her job were being terminated at the end of the year, she just might.

Jacqueline didn't get back to the office until the end of the day. Gregory was already gone when she got there. She assumed he'd already left to pack for his trip back east for the holiday. Hoping to catch him at home, she hurriedly cleared her desk. Gregory walked in just as she turned off her computer. She looked up. Her heart lifted. He was still here. "Hi."

"Hi." He crossed the room and dropped his briefcase on the desk, then perched on the edge facing her.

"You're here. I thought I missed you."

"No, but I missed you, all weekend," he said lovingly. "Are you and I not okay?"

She nodded. "We're okay." She crossed the room and closed the office door, then came back and stood at his desk. "That's what I want to talk to you about. I'm going to break our promise and talk about us for a few minutes."

"Jacqueline, I'm sorry I hurt you, but there was no other choice. I had to help the city. I love you," he said tenderly, "I do, but I couldn't be selfish and sacrifice the city."

"I know. I understand. And I'm glad you helped Paradise. You were right before. I am scared. I'm scared of being loved, scared of not being loved and scared of not being able to tell you that I love you."

"Jacqueline..."

She moved closer to him. "Everybody I've loved leaves me and I'm left to have to start over with a new plan. I didn't want to love you, Gregory, but I do and I am scared of what that means."

Greg smiled. "I love you, Jacqueline," he whispered quietly. "Nothing and no one will change that. Not even you."

She smiled near tears and nodded. "I love you, too."

"I know you're scared and I understand your feelings, but I need you to see me and not all that other stuff holding you back. It's not about Friday the thirteenth or superstitions or even destiny. It's about us, only us. I need you to trust me. Okay?"

She nodded. "Okay," she said, truly believing him.

He smiled, satisfied. "Now, I need to kiss you."

"No, not here," she said, looking around.

He stood quickly and pulled her into his arms. "Too bad." He kissed her. The instant their mouths touched she knew everything was perfect. "Come with me to D.C. and New York."

"I can't. I have a ton of work to do before the New Year."

"Two days without you," he said, pulling her into his arms again. "It's gonna seem like forever." He kissed her hand.

"You're coming back on Christmas day, right?"

"I'm gonna do my best."

"You'd better do better than that. I'll be waiting."

"Well, the door is closed. We don't have to wait."

"Okay, okay, enough of that. I need to get out of here and you have a flight to catch, don't you?" she said.

"My flight isn't for a while. My grandfather's picking mother up in LA then stopping here to get me."

"Well, in that case," she said seductively. She didn't need to finish the statement. They were both thinking the same thing. They went to her place and made love.

Chapter 17

Christmas day was amazing. The entire block was awash and glowing with colored lights and festive lawn decorations. It looked amazing. Jacqueline invited Tasha and friends over for an early holiday dinner. She had decorated her condo with lights and a large fully ornamented and tinseled evergreen. Twinkling white lights sparkled and shimmered around the room, and a dozen large, red poinsettia plants accented her living room and dining room. A sense of excitement had filled the air all day. She loved the holidays and the spirit of renewal they inspired. This was the one time of year she loved.

Since she was a teenager, having fun wasn't exactly top on her things-to-do list. With her mother gone and their father gambling constantly, it was left to her to be responsible. And that responsibility meant taking care of her eleven-year-old sister and making sure they had a stable home.

She hadn't minded that her dreams for her own future were set aside, replaced by the reality and sacrifice of day-to-day living. She had made a pretty good life for herself and her sister. Perhaps it wasn't a perfect life, but it was secure and there was love and that was all that mattered in the end.

After a long day of fun, laughter and excitement, Jacqueline walked Tasha to her car. They stood talking about the fun and craziness of the day. "I think everyone had a great time," Jacqueline said.

"They did," Tasha confirmed. "Especially Roger."

Jacqueline laughed. "I've never seen him so animated."

"He's a wild man," Tasha said. "What exactly was he doing, a jig?"

"I don't know what it was, but it was strange."

"No, what was strange was the robot, the worm and the moonwalk. I thought I was going to pee my pants."

The sisters laughed heartily. "I thought Bethany was going to bust a gut when he lowered that turkey into the hot oil."

"With all that spattering, what were we thinking?" she asked.

"Everything came out okay and we didn't burn the neighborhood down. And the turkey tasted great." They laughed again, reminiscing about her constantly checking the thermostat and propane tank as Bethany stood by, holding tight to the fire extinguisher. "And you, walking around with those massive heatproof gloves, clumsily trying to pick up the whole turkey with the metal tongs."

"It was heavier than I expected," she said, laughing hysterically in her defense.

"We'll know better next time," Tasha vowed.

"Next time, no way," Jacqueline said, as they laughed again.

"It's a shame Greg missed the fun," Tasha said, seeing Jacqueline smile. "And look at you, standing there holding Lucky in your arms. You two were inseparable all day. I still can't believe you agreed to take care of him."

"I know. Crazy, right?" she said.

"I never thought I'd see the day, you standing here holding a black cat in your arms. It must be love."

"It is," she said.

Tasha nodded smiling. "I knew it." She reached out and hugged her sister. "I knew it. You're perfect together."

"How do you know we're perfect together? You've only seen us together one time."

"Bethany told me."

"Bethany, what does she know about it?" Jacqueline asked.

"She knows that you've been seeing each other since the mayor's birthday reception," Tasha said.

"Oh no. If Bethany knows, the whole office knows."

"No, she only told me. She swore. She didn't even tell Roger. Nobody knows. Jac, I'm so happy for you." They hugged tightly again. "Now, I've got to get going. I'll call you later. Merry Christmas."

"It's supposed to rain tonight, so drive carefully.

Merry Christmas." Jacqueline waved as her sister got into the car and drove off. As soon as the car started Lucky jumped down and ran back to the vestibule. Jacqueline went back up to her condo, opened the door and waited a few seconds for Lucky to catch up. "So, what do we do for the rest of the night, Lucky?" She turned on some jazz music and dimmed the lights, leaving the Christmas tree lights to twinkle and shine brightly.

Lucky strolled over to the balcony doors and sat down. Jacqueline walked over and looked out. "Yeah, I miss him, too." She opened the sliding door and stepped outside. Lucky stayed curled up on the warming pad Gregory had given him. She walked to the rail and looked up at the darkened sky covered by heavy storm clouds. There was a flash of lightning in the distance, then a low rumble of thunder.

She looked down, thinking about Gregory. Everything reminded her of him. She was remembering their last time together right before he left. She was on top. She had impaled herself onto his hard penis and was sitting up, arched back and erect. Her hands were behind her on his thighs. She was riding him slow and easy, rocking up and down. He massaged her breasts, toying and tantalizing her nipples. Then he pulled her closer. She leaned in with her breasts teasing his face. He pressed them together and feasted, licking and suckling as she moved her hips faster and faster. The unimaginable climax that followed still made her shudder inside. She closed her eyes and shook her head. This was going to be impossible.

They hadn't talked about it, but she hoped and prayed he had changed his mind about leaving Paradise. The wind picked up. She wrapped her arms around her body, wishing he was there with her. After a while, it started to drizzle, then rain. She went back inside and closed the door. Lucky looked up lazily from his resting place. "It looks like a storm is coming fast. I think we need a drink, what do you think?" she asked. The lights went off then came back on a few seconds later.

She grabbed a flashlight just in case. It wasn't unusual for the lights to go out and stay out all night. She went into the kitchen and poured herself a glass of wine and for Lucky a saucer of milk. She placed the milk down on the kitchen floor. Lucky followed and began lapping up the milk. As she picked up her wine she instantly remembered her first night with Gregory. She glanced at the counter where she sat. The feeling of fullness was overwhelming. The lights flashed again. This time they didn't come back on.

Jacqueline grabbed her drink and the flashlight and headed back into the living room. The Christmas tree was still illuminated, since she had used her battery-operated surge protector to plug all the lights in. She looked out the side window. All the lights in the neighborhood were out. She was sure there was no way Gregory would be back tonight.

As soon as she sat down there was a knock on her door. She opened it. Greg stood there, smiling. He dropped his bag on the outside landing. As soon as she opened her mouth to speak, he stepped in and swept her up into his arms. His mouth covered hers instantly. The kiss was pure, heated passion. Force met force; their lips crushed together in a fierce coupling of desire and hunger. He ravaged her and she loved it. She wrapped her arms around his neck and held tight. They weren't going to make it to the bed or the bedroom. The kiss continued until neither could breathe.

"You're here," she rasped breathlessly. "I didn't think you'd make it with the storm and power outage."

"I'm here. I made it."

"Merry Christmas. Welcome home."

"I missed you. Two days was too long to be away from you." He groaned, holding tight, kissing her repeatedly: her neck, her shoulders and her lips. She laughed happily.

"Wait, you're getting me wet," she said.

He smiled seductively. "Yeah, that's the whole idea."

She giggled. "No, I mean your jacket is wet." He nodded and took it off. She grabbed it and tossed it on the chair by the door.

He licked his lips and nodded. "You look good enough to eat. And I'm one starving man." The seductive glint in his eyes made her blush. She knew exactly what he was thinking, and it wasn't about food. He reached for the top button on her shirt.

"Starving, huh?" She smiled coyly, then took a step back just out of his reach. He missed, but tried again. She stepped back once more. "Well, if you're starving, I have some leftover fried turkey in the refrigerator and some—" he stepped closer and grasped her shirt. He easily slipped the top button loose, then began with the others as she kept moving backward "—salad and potatoes and some—" she smiled as he fumbled clumsily with the last button "—dessert." A second later she stood in the center of the living room with her shirt wide open. He licked his lips. "Um, now this is what I call a welcome-home meal." He fingered the voluptuous swell of her breasts, still encased by the lace bra. Then he stopped and looked into her eyes. The fire in his eyes and the intensity in his voice stirred her heart. "I love you with every part of my mind, my spirit and my body, always and forever."

She felt his words seep deep into her soul. She knew this wasn't just lustful passion or horizontal promises. She stepped closer and wrapped her arms around his neck, her heart pounding thunderously. She knew the thrill of their love was all she'd ever need. No more coy games, no more caution, no more fear. She wanted him as much as he wanted her. He was hers and she was his. "I love you too, so much, always and forever."

The kiss was slow but immediate, and everything inside of them exploded. Unrestrained passion surged in vigorous intent. He held her tight, kissing and touching her body possessively. She closed her eyes and gasped at the mind-boggling sensation of his love. Stroking, thrusting, longing hunger soared. They were completely enthralled by their passion as he dropped to his knees to kiss her stomach, her hips, her thighs...

There was a flash of light and a loud clap of thunder sounded. She opened her eyes and saw a black flash run out the open door. "Lucky, no!" she called out, and without thinking grabbed the flashlight and ran after him. Greg turned, seeing Jacqueline hurry after the cat. He followed.

"Jacqueline, wait." She was halfway down the steps and headed for the pathway. "Jacqueline."

"Lucky!" she called out again, and hurried out into the pouring rain. By the time she got to the driveway the cat was nowhere in sight. She looked around the cars and then down the street flashing around the light steadily. It was complete darkness. "Lucky!" she called out.

"Jacqueline," Greg said, catching up with her. He grabbed her arm to stop her from going farther down the street. She turned. She was completely soaked. "Come back inside. Lucky's okay, come on."

She looked at him and shook her head. "He ran out. I'm sorry. He just ran out the open door."

"It's okay, come on inside. He's probably drier than you are right now." She nodded and followed him back up to her condo. She spared one last glance in hope of seeing him. "Come on. Let's get you dry."

Greg closed the front door, still holding on to her hand. He pulled her into his embrace and kissed her tenderly, taking up where they'd left off. Her clothes stuck to her body, and he was even more enticed by the sight of her in the dim lighting. "I need a towel."

"No, you don't," he said. He kissed her again. This time the kiss was tender and lasting. His mouth lowered to her neck and shoulders as he removed her shirt and tossed it with his jacket. He'd been hard earlier just seeing her. Now, seeing her skin wet and glistening against the tree's lights had him desperately struggling to keep control. He licked the wet from her neck and shoulders then tasted the dampness on her chest. He unzipped her pants and helped them to the carpet and onto the chair.

She stood in just bra, panties and a smile. The twinkling Christmas lights continuously sparkled off the dampness of her body. She seemed to shimmer. He ran his open palm down the front of her. She held her breath when he touched her stomach then went lower. "You are stunning."

"I bet you say that to all the wet women you undress."

"As far as I'm concerned, there are no other women."

She unfastened his belt and pulled his shirt free. She unbuttoned it and let it drop. He removed the rest of his clothes, then leaned in and kissed her earlobe. "Wait here, don't move." He quickly disappeared into her bedroom and returned with condoms. He put one on, then knelt down in front of her and held her waist. He unsnapped her bra, kissed her stomach and slowly removed her panties.

She was his and he was hers. His mouth and his hands touched her everywhere. She gasped and moaned and shrieked and cried out in pleasure. After he'd explored his fill, he lay back beneath the tree. She climbed on top, impaling herself onto his hard shaft. She pressed her hips in and out, as they made slow, sultry, sensuous, lasting love beneath the starry lights.

Afterward, she nodded off and woke up lying in her own bed. Greg was gone. She got up and looked around. The clock on the side table was blinking. The lights were back on. She walked through the living room and found him standing outside on the balcony looking out at the clearing skies. "Hey, what are you doing out here?"

He turned and smiled, seeing her. "I'm waiting for you."

"Why didn't you wake me?"

"You were sleeping too soundly, and I love to watch you."

"You really need to get a hobby," she joked.

"I have one—you."

She smiled as she walked up beside him. He wrapped

her in his arms and held her close. "I love the smell after the rain. It looks like the storm has passed," she said. "The electricity is back on." She heard a purring sound and looked around. "Lucky's back."

"Yes, he was hiding in the bushes by my front door."

"Good. I'm glad he's okay."

"Jacqueline, come inside. I need to talk to you."

"I have a feeling I'm not going to like whatever you need to tell me."

She sat down. He sat beside her. "My contract here is pretty much finished. I have a few things to take care of, but basically I'm done."

Jacqueline's heart quivered. This was it. She knew it would be coming. He was leaving and everything between them was over. "You're leaving again," she said, not giving him a chance to say the words.

"Yes, I have to go back to D.C. to take care of some business, and I was offered a job there. I'd like you to go with me, as my wife. Will you marry me, Jacqueline?"

"Gregory, wait, what?" She was shocked.

"Jacqueline, I'm asking you to marry me, to be my wife."

"And live in D.C.? I can't. My life is here. I can't leave."

"Yes, you can. We can drive to Las Vegas tonight, get married and fly to D.C. tomorrow morning. Afterward we'll have any wedding you plan. The sky's the limit."

"But I can't. I have the celebration to work on still."

"You already have mostly everything set for the New Year's celebration. You can call from D.C. about anything else that needs your attention."

"And what about the event itself?" she asked.

"We'll fly back for that. Marry me. Say yes."

"No. Gregory, I can't just pack up my whole life and leave Paradise just like that. What about my job here?" she asked, and then realized she didn't have one anymore.

"You don't have a job here," he said.

"No, still, I can't. I can't. I'm sorry." She stood and walked away.

"Jacqueline…" He walked over to her.

She turned. "Stay here with me."

"I can't."

"Then I guess that's it."

He nodded. She turned away. A few minutes later she heard her front door open and close. She turned back. He was gone.

Chapter 18

It was early still, but the buzz of excitement was already all over the city. Jacqueline went into the office her last day not expecting to see many people there. As she'd thought, the place was quiet and practically empty. She had had her goodbye party and did all the hugging the day before. Today was just for last-minute details and finishing up her end report.

For Jacqueline, the last week had flown by in a blur of passionless activity. She continued to do her job, keeping to herself in joyless dedication to the position she no longer held. She worked, but her heart was still so heavy. To her surprise, it wasn't about the job she was losing. It was about the man she'd lost. Still, she focused everything she had left on her last event. She intended for it to be the best ever.

Seeing Greg hadn't been the problem she expected.

Thankfully he spent most of his time in meetings with the mayor and the city council. When he was around, which was seldom, they made sure to focus exclusively on business. He spent most of her last week working feverishly on the last of the city's wayward finances.

It was done. Jacqueline was headed out for the last time. She had cleared out her desk and turned over her final report, leaving everything neatly for Greg to review. Having put everything else in the car, she grabbed her cell and her purse and stood to leave.

"Hello."

Jacqueline looked up and saw Tasha standing in the doorway. Tasha walked over to her sister's cleared desk.

"Hey, what are you doing here?" Jacqueline asked.

Tasha smiled. "I thought you could use some help." They hugged, then Tasha looked around. "Looks like you're all set."

Bethany knocked on the door and hurried in. "Hey, did you hear the news about the scholarships?"

"No. What's wrong now?" she asked.

"Nothing, it's great news. Some foundation gave each student a seventeen-hundred-dollar scholarship. So with the city's three hundred dollars, they'll each get a two-thousand-dollar award. That's double the usual."

Jacqueline was so overjoyed she nearly cried. "That's wonderful news. I know the kids are happy."

"Yeah, they're crazy excited," Tasha said.

"Calls have been coming in all morning. Everybody wants to know the name of the foundation," Bethany added.

"What *is* the name of the foundation?" Tasha asked.

"I don't know. Greg said it was an anonymous donation."

"I bet he did," Jacqueline said, knowing he gave the money.

"So, you ready to go?" Tasha asked.

"Yep, just taking one last look around," she said.

"Do you know what you're gonna do yet?" Bethany asked.

Jacqueline nodded. "Yes, I'm going to open up my own special-events business."

"Excellent. Can I come to work for you?" Tasha asked.

"Oh, me too, me too," Bethany added excitedly.

"I'm gonna be bare-bones for a while. I'm still waiting to hear about a loan I applied for. But yes, you're both hired. There are a million things to do and I have no idea where or how I'm going to get clients."

"Oh, that's easy," Bethany said. "I have a feeling you'll be back soon."

Bethany moved closer to speak quietly. "I heard that Greg suggested the city hire you as special-events consultant."

"Cool, that's your first client already," Tasha said.

Bethany nodded. "Yeah, now you get to do the fun stuff without dealing with the dumb stuff, plus you'll have other clients, too."

"Other clients? Maybe I better rethink this," Jacqueline joked.

"I heard Uncle Leland tell Aunt Peggy that the State Tourism Division was headed your way, too. They're a huge contract."

Tasha laughed excitedly. "You'd better get up and running fast, Jac. Next year is going to be busy. You always said you were going to open up your own business one of these days. I guess that day is today."

"I guess it was a good thing after all that the department closed and I'm leaving here."

"You're not the only one leaving," Bethany said.

"Who else is leaving?" Tasha asked.

"Someone from the U.S. Office of Personnel Management called earlier to speak to Uncle Leland. It was about Greg working in D.C. again."

They both looked at Jacqueline. "I know. He told me the day after Christmas."

"Jacqueline, I'm so sorry," Tasha said.

"Me, too," Bethany added.

Jacqueline's heart sank. She looked over at his desk. "Bethany, do you know where Greg is now? I haven't seen him all day."

"He's back in D.C. I think he left last night."

Jacqueline's world staggered sideways. The empty feeling of loss swept through her instantly. She stood there, silent. He was gone. She had refused him and pushed him away. Suddenly, leaving Paradise to live in D.C. didn't seem so terrible anymore. After all, she'd have Gregory. What else could she possibly need?

"So, everybody ready for tonight? Everything set?" Tasha said, hoping to lighten the mood in the room.

"I'm ready," Bethany said.

"Bethany, Tasha, thanks for everything. I'll see you out there tonight. I gotta go." She hugged them both, then left.

Jacqueline went directly to Greg's condo. She knocked and rang the bell, but there was no answer. She considered calling, but what she had to say she needed to say in person. It was getting late and she still had one more job to do. She went up to her place, packed, made arrangements, changed and then headed to the open site of the New Year's celebration.

She worked steadily, checking and rechecking all details. By evening the mayor and his wife had arrived, and so had a select number of special guests, including the city council. Tasha and Bethany helped, and so did Roger and everyone else from the city office. Everything was running smoothly.

It was the last day of the year, and an infectious celebratory mood was all around. Everyone was exhilarated and anticipating a wondrous event. Thousands and thousands of spectators had begun to gather from all across the county and state. The word was out and excitement filled the air. Earlier that afternoon dozens of hot air balloon companies had come to participate in the first annual Paradise New Year's Night Glow Celebration.

The sun hung low in the sky and spread wide across the mountainous terrain. The night was warm, and the sky was crystal clear. The magic of anticipation was all around. Preparations were intense, and Jacqueline was right in the midst of everything. Floodlights surrounded the main stage as Mayor Leland Newbury stood to welcome the numerous special guests. It looked as if all of Paradise and its surrounding cities showed up. Even the state's governor attended. They each spoke briefly. Then the musical entertainment began.

The audience danced and sang and held hands, all celebrating the coming new year. As the night sky descended, everything was set for the final show. The mayor spoke and the burners were turned on. The fans began blowing hot air into the envelopes. The massive balloons began to slowly but steadily rise up off the ground. Everyone watched in awe as the music began and the floodlights dimmed. There was near silence.

Then, on cue, a mass of vibrant colors radiated brilliantly across the landscape. The audience gasped in unison, then applauded. The sight was breathtaking and magnificent. The entire regatta of one hundred balloons had not shown up, but the thirty or so that did made the night unimaginably memorable. The phenomenal night glow continued as the year drew to an end.

Ten main balloons, located slightly away from the others, readied themselves for the final presentation. Each hovered barely off the ground, preparing for the final countdown. This had been Jacqueline's main focus. She kept in constant contact via cell phone with the main stage, but she had opted to be with the countdown balloons. Everything was set. It was almost time. Jacqueline kept watch near the main balloon. She had hoped Greg would have come. She was sure he'd love this.

"Is it always this exciting being backstage?"

She turned and saw Greg behind her. "Greg," she said, smiling, then grabbed and hugged him. "You're here. You came."

"Of course. I wouldn't miss this for the world."

"But what are you doing here? I thought you left."

"You're not getting rid of me that easily. I love you and that's for always and forever. This is a destiny thing now, remember." He kissed her lips tenderly. Her heart was beating so hard she could barely breathe.

"Wait, but I heard you were back in D.C."

"I was. I needed to take care of some business, like selling my house there. I passed on the job offer. It was an incredible opportunity, one that doesn't come along every day. But I already have the opportunity of a lifetime, right here, loving you. So, now I'm here for good. Paradise is my home."

She laughed happily. "Then I guess I'd better cancel my flight to D.C. tomorrow morning."

He laughed and nodded. "Definitely. I guess we're both gonna need jobs after tonight."

"Maybe I'll think about hiring you," she joked. He looked at her, puzzled. "I got a loan to open my own business."

"That's wonderful, perfect."

"Thank you."

"For what? You all did this."

"Thank you for laying me off and starting my client list. Welcome home," she said softly. They kissed again and those standing around applauded them. Jacqueline laughed as Greg held her close.

He looked around. "This is phenomenal. You did an incredible job."

She nodded. "Can I plan, or can I plan?" she said proudly.

"Sweetheart, you can most certainly plan. But I can, too."

"What do you mean?" she asked curiously.

"Come on, we'd better hurry."

"I can't, I need to be here. It's almost time for the finale."

"You're right. It is almost time." He took her hand and started walking.

"What are you doing?" she asked.

"No questions. Come on."

He hurried them over to the center balloon. The pilot

and his assistants seemed to be waiting for them. "All set?" Greg asked.

The pilot nodded. "Welcome aboard, folks."

"Wait, I can't go up there. I have to—"

He picked her up and placed her in the large basket. "You have to be exactly where you are." He hopped in quickly.

The woven basket was huge inside. There was easily enough room for twenty people.

"Do you have any idea what you're doing?" she asked.

"I know exactly what I'm doing."

"Are we actually going up?"

"It's your finale. Your plan."

He was right. This was her finale. Ten balloons would slowly rise as the ten-second countdown proceeded. The other balloons were already up several feet off the ground. The center balloon would go the highest and glow steadily at the stroke of midnight. "I can't believe I'm doing this. It's not the plan."

"It's my plan," Greg said, holding her close.

The pilot tossed out a drop line. Four assistants grabbed hold and anchored it as the balloon began to rise up. Jacqueline held tight to Gregory as the balloon ascended. Soon they were far off the ground and looking down onto the festivities. What little wind there was was calm and placid.

"It's so beautiful up here. I never imagined it could be like this."

"I can say the same thing about being with you. When I came here just a few weeks ago I never thought I'd meet someone like you. I love you, Jacqueline."

She smiled up into his sparkling eyes. "I love you,

too. I can't fight it anymore. The moment I saw you, I knew you'd change my life. I was just too scared to admit it, but not anymore. Meeting you on Friday the thirteenth was the luckiest day of my life."

"Mine, too."

Then, moments before twelve o'clock, everything went dark. The balloons hovered in readiness, each strategically in place to form an arch of color to the sky. As the crowd below began counting down from ten seconds the balloons began to burn. Each lighting the flame as the seconds passed.

"I brought something back from D.C. for you."

"What?"

"This." He took her hand and placed a square-cut platinum-set diamond ring on her ring finger.

She gasped. She stared at the ring and then at him. "Greg."

"Jacqueline, you're an amazing woman. I knew the instant I saw you you were special. I fought it, but you were my destiny. I need you in my life, now and forever. I adore you, I cherish you, I love you with all my heart and soul. Will you be my wife? Will you marry me?"

She shook her head. "I don't know what to say."

"Say yes."

She smiled happily. "Yes, yes, yes."

He kissed her, and the balloon lit up on cue at the stroke of midnight. The people down below went wild, screaming and applauding. Jacqueline expected the jubilant celebration, but nothing like what was going on now. She looked out at the crowd below. A spotlight centered on their basket. Greg waved and the crowd went wild again. Mayor Newbury read what Greg had given him earlier. "Ladies and gentlemen, she said yes."

Jacqueline laughed and waved. Tears flowed like water. "I can't believe you planned all this."

"Your destiny will come true when you're on top of the world," he said.

"What did you say?" she asked.

"That's what my fortune cookie said that night at the restaurant."

She laughed and nodded. "Mine did, too."

He held her tight and they kissed, welcoming the New Year with a love that was destined to last forever.

* * * * *